D0683913

The Love Vow

Brittany's heart had never flipped for any boy the way it had for Tim Cooper. He was The One, she was sure. If she had him, her life would be every bit as magical as she wanted it to be.

She wanted him. Now all she had to do was get him to want her. She didn't know how she would manage that but she was sure she'd find a way. She always did.

Brittany tossed her magazine aside and sat up, her teeth clenched in determination. One thing was certain: no way was she going to let Nikki Masters walk off with Tim Cooper. If she had to fight, then so be it. She'd fight—and win.

Most Archway Paperbacks are available at special quantity discounts for bulk purchases for sales promotions, premiums or fund raising. Special books or book excerpts can also be created to fit specific needs.

For details write the office of the Vice President of Special Markets, Pocket Books, 1230 Avenue of the Americas, New York, New York 10020.

RI#1VER
HEIGHTS

LOVE
TIMES THREE

C A R O L Y N
K E E N E

AN ARCHWAY PAPERBACK
Published by POCKET BOOKS
New York   London   Toronto   Sydney   Tokyo

This book is a work of fiction. Names, character, places and
incidents are either the product of the author's imagination or
are used fictitiously. Any resemblance to actual events or locales
or persons, living or dead, is entirely coincidental.

AN ARCHWAY PAPERBACK *Original*

An Archway Paperback published by
POCKET BOOKS, a division of Simon & Schuster Inc.
1230 Avenue of the Americas, New York, NY 10020

Copyright © 1989 by Simon & Schuster Inc.
Cover art copyright © 1989 Peter Caras
Logo art copyright © 1989 James Mathewuse
Produced by Mega-Books of New York, Inc.

All rights reserved, including the right to reproduce
this book or portions thereof in any form whatsoever.
For information address Pocket Books, 1230 Avenue
of the Americas, New York, NY 10020

ISBN: 0-671-67759-4

First Archway Paperback printing September 1989

10 9 8 7 6 5 4 3 2 1

RIVER HEIGHTS® is a trademark of
Simon & Schuster Inc.

Printed in the U.S.A.

IL 6+

LOVE
TIMES THREE

~~ Prologue

"Do you want my honest opinion, Nikki?" Nancy Drew tilted her head, her red-gold hair swinging to one side, and gave her next-door neighbor a long, critical look. Then her face broke into a wide grin. "I think you're going to knock the socks off every boy at River Heights High!"

Sixteen-year-old Nicola Masters—Nikki for short—laughed and shook her head. "I'm not so sure about that, but thanks for the compliment," she said, returning Nancy's grin. "I just asked if you thought this outfit was okay for the first day of school."

"And I just told you it's more than okay." Putting her hands on Nikki's shoulders,

Nancy spun her friend around so that she was facing the full-length mirror on the back of Nancy's bedroom door. "There," Nancy said emphatically. "Take a good look at yourself and then tell me I'm exaggerating!"

Nikki stepped up to study her image in the mirror. Shiny, medium-length blond hair framed her gently rounded face. Her azure blue sweater exactly matched her long-lashed eyes and made· the most of her perfectly proportioned figure. So did her skirt, a straight shaft of winter white cotton that buttoned down the front and stopped just short of her knees, revealing her slim, lightly tanned legs.

"Well?" Nancy asked.

"Well . . ." Nikki shrugged, then nodded at her reflection. "I might not turn the male population of River Heights High into a bunch of raving maniacs, but you're right, Nancy. I do look okay."

"You look great," Nancy corrected her firmly as she started rummaging in one of her desk drawers.

While Nancy was busy at her desk, Nikki glanced around the room. Nancy was eighteen, and her bedroom looked like a typical teenager's. Jeans and a sweatshirt were draped over a chair, a poster of a rock star decorated one· wall, and records and tapes were piled high next to the stereo.

But Nancy Drew was more than a typical teenager. She was also a famous detective who had solved countless baffling mysteries, and her bedroom reflected that, too. Amid the clutter of makeup and photos on Nancy's dresser sat an odd-looking antique clock. It was, Nikki knew, a souvenir from the case that had launched Nancy's career as a detective. And though Nancy's four-drawer file cabinet was bright pink, its contents were mysteriously labeled:

(A)rson – (J)udo
(K)idnapping – (P)oison
(Q)uestioning Techniques – (S)uspects
(T)elephone Codes – (Z)oom Lenses

Even now, seeing that file cabinet was enough to send a shiver down Nikki's spine. Just a short time ago, her own name had probably been in there. Under *M*. Not for *"Masters"*—for *"murder."*

"Listen, Nikki," Nancy said, turning around to face Nikki and breaking into her thoughts. "I know it's not like you to be so unsure of yourself and worried about how you look. And I know why you're nervous. It's because you're afraid people will still be gossiping." Nancy looked Nikki straight in the eye. "Just remember—I caught the real killer so your name is completely clear."

"I know, and I am grateful," Nikki said, but she couldn't help sighing a little. It was bad enough that the boy she'd been dating, Dan Taylor, had been killed. But when she'd become the number-one murder suspect, her life had turned into a nightmare. If it hadn't been for Nancy, Nikki was sure she'd be on trial right then, instead of worrying about her back-to-school wardrobe.

"I don't really think anyone still believes I'm guilty," she added. "But people *do* give me funny looks. And I've heard them whispering when they think I can't hear. They'll do it at school, too, I know they will." She shivered and then laughed ruefully. "I guess it's not exactly the best way to start my junior year."

Nancy nodded thoughtfully. People *did* love to gossip, even when there wasn't anything to gossip about. Since Nikki's family was well-known—one of the wealthiest and most prominent in River Heights—any gossip about her was even juicier. But she couldn't afford to let it get her down, or her whole school year *would* be a disaster.

"Listen," Nancy said, standing up and putting a small gift-wrapped box on her desk. She walked over to put her arm around Nikki. "The worst part is over. You're right. Some people will probably talk and give you weird looks—until something more interesting comes up. Then you'll be old news."

Nikki smiled. "I'd give anything to be old news right now."

"It'll happen," Nancy assured her. "But what are you going to do until it does?"

"I guess"—Nikki hesitated—"I'll ignore the whispers and funny looks, right?"

"Right!" Nancy said as if Nikki had just passed a test. "Remember, you're not Nikki Masters, suspect. You're Nikki Masters, bright student, talented photographer, loyal friend. And don't forget," she added, her blue eyes sparkling, "great-looking girl."

Nikki was laughing by now. She felt better than she had in ages.

"And in case you do start to forget," Nancy went on, crossing to her desk and picking up the small box, "I got you this to remind yourself." She thrust the present into Nikki's hands and stood back to watch her open it.

Nikki tore off the pretty silver paper and lifted the lid off the box. Inside, on a bed of cotton, lay a beautiful ballpoint pen, striped in vivid rainbow colors. On one side, in gold lettering, were the initials *N. M.*

"I'm sure you've already bought your school supplies," Nancy said, "but I figure you could always use an extra pen."

"I love it," Nikki replied. "Thanks, Nancy. I'll take down my very first assignment with it tomorrow." She grinned. "You make a good one-member fan club."

"I'm glad you like the pen," Nancy told her. "But remember, your fan club has more than one member. Your family, your friends —they're behind you all the way, too."

"I won't forget," Nikki promised. "In fact," she said firmly, "I'm going to make my junior year the best year ever!"

1

"Nikki, over here!" Lacey Dupree waved and motioned for Nikki to join her. "I saved you a seat!"

Smiling, Nikki made her way down the aisle of the school bus toward her best friend. It was Tuesday, the first day of school, and Nikki had been up since five-thirty. She had been too excited to sleep a single minute longer.

The bus was filled with voices buzzing in a dozen different conversations, but when Nikki was halfway to Lacey, she heard one girl say clearly, "Nikki Masters, well, you know what she did." For a split second all the talking stopped, and all heads swiveled toward Nikki. She felt a flush spread up her neck and across her cheeks. The gossip she'd dreaded was starting already.

Remember, she told herself, it won't last forever. Nikki raised her chin and kept on walking. "You look great!" Lacey said as Nikki sat down. "I love that sweater. The blue is perfect with your eyes." Lowering her voice, she added, "I know you were dying when you heard that girl's remark just now, but you acted completely cool."

"Thanks," Nikki said, "but I didn't feel very cool. I hope I can keep up the act."

"You probably won't have to," Lacey told her. "By the time we get to school, everybody'll be too busy trying to figure out where the first class is to think about you or anything else."

The remark was typical of Lacey, who was always optimistic and a true romantic. She looked the part of a romantic that day with her ruffled white blouse, cameo, and full, calf-length floral-print skirt. Her long, wavy red hair was pulled back into a thick braid, but a few curls had escaped, framing her pale face, which was dusted with freckles. Her light blue eyes usually had a faraway look in them, but Lacey's mind was in perfect working order. She got good grades, had been voted junior class secretary, and held down an after-school job at a record store.

Nikki felt her spirits rising. "We're juniors

at last!'' she said. "This is the year we've all been waiting for.''

"It's going to be great!'' Lacey agreed excitedly. "I still can't believe I'm class secretary. Between that and my job, I'm going to be swamped.''

"You forgot a few little things, Lacey. Like trig and English and chemistry,'' Nikki pointed out wryly.

"And boys,'' Lacey added significantly. "I have a feeling this is going to be *the* year for love.''

Nikki hoped so—for Lacey's sake, at least. For herself, well, love was just a word now. After all, she had thought she was madly in love with Dan Taylor, but she'd been wrong.

Dan was the first boy Nikki had ever really cared about, and after what had happened, she wasn't ready to trust her judgment. One of these days she'd be ready to fall in love again, but for now she planned to steer clear of romance and work hard as a photographer for the River Heights *Record,* the student newspaper.

A gasp from Lacey interrupted her thoughts. "Am I seeing straight?'' Lacey cried. "No, I must be dreaming!''

"What is it?'' Nikki asked, hiding a smile. Lacey usually *was* dreaming.

"A boy I just saw,'' Lacey said, her face

pressed against the bus window. "I could swear it was Rick Stratton!"

Nikki peered over Lacey's shoulder. The bus had pulled into the high school drive, which was crowded with kids in cars, on bikes, and on foot. She couldn't pick out anyone in particular. "Okay," she asked, "why couldn't it have been Rick?"

"Because he's a scrawny scarecrow. But this guy"—Lacey shook her head, her eyes wide—"he was a hunk!"

"Maybe Rick took a bodybuilding course over the summer," Nikki suggested. Then she laughed. "It's kind of hard to imagine Rick Stratton pumping iron, though."

"Besides, the guy I saw was getting out of a car. I don't think Rick has a car." Lacey sighed. "I wish *I* did. If I save every penny from my job, and if I don't buy a single new thing to wear for the entire school year, do you think I could save enough to get one?"

Nikki shrugged. "It's worth a try." A car *would* be great, she thought. Her grandfather, who had started the highly successful Masters Electronics, which Nikki's father now owned and operated, had offered to buy her one. Nikki's parents had thanked him but said they wanted to think about it. Nikki hoped they were thinking positively.

But as the bus jolted to a stop, Nikki forgot all about cars. The first day of school was about to begin. Nikki's heart was thumping with excitement as she and Lacey joined the swirling crowd streaming toward the school.

The neoclassical North Wing of River Heights High, built many years before, had wide marble steps leading to its entrance. The classrooms were large, with high ceilings and tall windows.

The South Wing, on the other hand, was very modern—early twenty-first century in style. A sprawling complex of "learning environments," it had red ventilation ducts snaking through the halls and green computer screens glowing in each room.

It was a beautiful September day, sunny and warm. The grass-covered quad was filled with hundreds of students shouting out greetings and catching up on news. As Nikki and Lacey made their way through the noisy, milling throng, Nikki couldn't help but notice all the curious glances she was getting. Several conversations stopped dead as she passed. Ben Newhouse, president of the junior class, bumped right into her and stammered out a greeting, his rugged face turning bright red.

"Hi, Ben," Nikki said, answering his hi. She'd never seen Ben blush before. "How was your summer?"

"Great, great!" Ben boomed with false heartiness. "How was yours?" His blush deepened as he realized the awkwardness of his question, and he started edging away. "Hey, listen, Nikki, great seeing you. Catch you later."

"Oh, Nikki," Lacey said sympathetically as Ben disappeared.

" 'Oh, Nikki' is right," Nikki said, pasting on a smile.

Just then she spotted a tall girl with short dark hair, huge dark eyes, and a turned-up nose. As soon as she caught sight of Nikki and Lacey, she grinned and thrust her hand into the air.

"Nikki! Lacey!" she yelled. "Over here!"

It was Robin Fisher, Nikki and Lacey's other best friend, and even if they hadn't seen her first, they wouldn't have needed much help in finding her. She was the swim team's most dedicated member, and she had a great figure to prove it. She also seemed to have an inside line on what was hot in the fashion industry. That day she was wearing black cycling pants, a man's white dress shirt, and hot pink high-tops.

"Quick!" Robin said as Nikki and Lacey approached. "Tell me where your home-rooms are. North or South?"

Nikki's computer printout of classes had arrived in the mail only the day before, and she had to consult it again. "North," she said. "Mrs. Sheedy."

"You're lucky," Lacey moaned. *"I* got stuck in South."

"What's wrong with South?" Robin demanded. "I'm in South, too, and I'm glad. North is such a pokey old building. Archaeologists are probably dying to get their hands on it."

"But it's beautiful," Lacey argued. "And South is a confusing maze. I'll need a map and compass just to find my way around."

"That's because you're such a space case, Lacey," Robin remarked, her dark eyes twinkling. "You'd probably need a map and compass to find your own bedroom."

"I most certainly would not!" Lacey tried to sound indignant, but she couldn't help giggling, too.

Nikki laughed, feeling much more comfortable now that she was with her two best friends. How Robin and Lacey had become friends, Nikki would never figure out. The two of them had totally opposite personalities: Lacey the dreamer and Robin the realist. But Nikki knew they'd always be there for each other—and for her.

As Lacey and Robin continued to argue the merits of North and South, Nikki looked around the quad. There was DeeDee Smith, the editor of the *Record*. And there was Jeremy Pratt, the rich, good-looking snob king of River Heights High. Robin called him

"Preppy Pratt" and looked as if she'd just bitten into a lemon whenever she said it. And over there, surrounded as always by a big group of admiring boys and laughing girls, was Brittany Tate.

Sensational was the word for Brittany. She had long, lustrous dark hair, gleaming dark eyes, a pretty full mouth, and a figure that curved beautifully beneath her clinging skirt and her silky blouse.

Brittany always attracted a crowd. The school's social queen bee, she headed up what seemed like a hundred clubs and committees and wrote the school paper's widely read column "Off the Record."

Nikki knew Brittany—but not well. Brittany's father was a senior engineer at Masters Electronics and had recently designed some new gizmo that Nikki's dad called revolutionary. Brittany was always polite to Nikki, but she was also cool and distant. Nikki sometimes got the feeling that Brittany was checking her out, studying the way she talked and dressed; other times, Brittany acted as if she didn't exist. Nikki couldn't decide whether the girl liked her or not.

Then Nikki's gaze fell on a nearby group of giggling girls, and she immediately forgot about Brittany. As soon as the girls saw Nikki looking their way, they fell silent. A few of them blushed. One girl, obviously new at River Heights High, asked a question, and Nikki heard the incredulous reply: "Why, that's Nikki Masters. You mean you don't *know?*"

Nikki felt her face grow hot again.

"Don't worry, Nikki," Lacey said softly. "Everything will work out, you'll see."

"Ha!" Robin's dark eyes were flashing. *"Some* people," she said loudly, looking straight at the group of girls, "are born dweebs, and dweebs never change." Her voice dropped. "Ignore them, Nik, they're hopeless."

Nikki took a deep breath and smiled at both of her friends. But inside, her spirits had taken a nosedive.

Meanwhile, across the quad, Brittany Tate dragged her eyes away from Nikki Masters and turned back to Ben Newhouse. "I'm sorry, Ben," she said sweetly. "What were you saying?"

"I asked if I could count on you," Ben told her. "You know, to help run the halftime show for the alumni football game. It **has** to be pretty spectacular."

"And *I* wanted to know if you'd started your first 'Off the Record' column yet," DeeDee Smith put in. "The deadline's coming up fast."

"I know that," Brittany said. Actually she had no idea when the deadline was. "Naturally I've started the column." Another lie, but DeeDee didn't have to know that. She'd get the column done in a flash—just as soon as she decided what to write about.

Brittany turned back to Ben. "And don't worry," she said. "The halftime show will be a knockout. I guarantee it."

With that settled, Brittany glanced at Nikki Masters. She hated to admit it, but the girl was handling things beautifully.

Suddenly Brittany frowned. Of course she's handling it, she thought irritably. With her background and upbringing, Nikki can afford to stay cool even if the entire junior class is whispering about her.

Brittany had worked and schemed hard to get to the top, and it made her furious to think that Nikki Masters had been born there. Not that her own family was poor, but life would be much easier if she didn't have to try so hard.

"Brittany!" Kim Bishop, Brittany's best friend, startled her from her thoughts. Everything about Kim was sharp—her voice, her nose, her cheekbones, her attitude. Blond and trim, she rivaled Jeremy Pratt for the title of School Snob. "When are you going to stop staring at Nikki?" she asked. "You're turning green, and it's not your best color."

"That's right." Samantha Daley nodded. A transplanted southern belle, Samantha was delicately pretty, with wide cinnamon-brown eyes, brown permed hair, and a lilting accent. There was nothing fragile about Samantha's mind, though. She could cook up schemes with the best of them. "Why don't you just forget about little old Nikki and listen to some really juicy news?"

They'll never understand, Brittany thought. But they were right about one thing. She'd been looking at Nikki for much too long. "Okay," she said. "I'm ready for some hot gossip. What is it?"

"There's a new guy in school," Samantha said, lowering her voice as if she were imparting a state secret. "I hear he's absolutely gorgeous!"

"I haven't seen him, either," Kim added briskly, "but his name's Tim Cooper. He wants to be an actor."

Samantha gave a throaty laugh. "Wouldn't it be fun to discover him?"

Brittany wasn't impressed. "If he's gorgeous, he's probably conceited," she stated flatly. "And if he wants to be an actor, he's crazy."

"Suit yourself," Samantha said with a lazy shrug. "But I plan to keep my eyes—and options—wide open."

The warning bell rang suddenly, and as

everyone started heading into the building, Brittany and her friends were separated. Brittany had to reassure Ben once again about the halftime show. Then she realized she had to hurry or she'd be late for home-room.

Dashing across the quad, Brittany looked down briefly at her watch and ran headlong into someone coming from the opposite di-rection. She fell backward and sprawled on the soft grass.

"I'm sorry!" a low voice said.

Sputtering indignantly, Brittany saw a male hand reach out to help her. She took it and looked up into the most startling gray eyes she'd ever seen. The guy's hand was warm and strong, his hair was dark and thick, and his build was sensational.

Brittany swallowed and finally found her voice. "It wasn't your fault," she told him with a bright smile. Who *was* this dream of masculine perfection? "It was mine. I wasn't looking where I was going."

"Well, I wasn't, either," he said. "I guess we're even."

They both laughed, and the boy turned away.

"Wait!" Brittany cried. She swallowed again and tried to sound casual, as if her heart weren't thudding in her ears like a drum. "We might as well introduce ourselves. I'm Brittany Tate."

She held out her hand, and he took it. "Tim Cooper," he said. "I'm new this year. Your name is Brittany?"

She nodded, reluctantly letting go of his hand.

"It's nice to meet you. Well, I guess I'd better get going," he added as the second bell rang. "But I'm sure I'll see you again, Brittany."

Oh, you *will*, Brittany thought as she watched him hurry off. Samantha and Kim had been right. And as of right now, Samantha's options were closed as far as Tim Cooper was concerned.

Brittany Tate was in love.

2 ⌒⌒⌒

After Nikki went to her locker, she had only two minutes to get to her homeroom, in 101 North. The halls were filled with jostling students, the freshmen looking panicked and the upperclassmen acting cool but moving quickly just the same. At least no one had time now to stare or whisper behind her back.

Room 101 was in a state of barely controlled pandemonium. Nikki could hear the shouting and laughter halfway down the hall. She carefully smoothed down her hair and walked inside just as the final bell rang.

Almost instantly the noise stopped. Twenty heads turned toward the door, and twenty pairs of eyes fastened on Nikki. The silence lasted only a second before the noise began to build again, but Nikki felt as if she'd been standing in the white-hot glare of a giant spotlight.

Nikki spotted an empty desk in the last row, in the far corner. It would be the perfect seat to hide out in, she thought, and headed toward it.

"Hey, Nikki," someone mumbled. It was Erik Nielson, the tall blond cocaptain of the cheerleading squad.

"Hey, Erik," Nikki practically whispered back. Erik was usually energetic and outgoing. He never mumbled, she knew, but then, neither did she.

Halfway to her desk, Nikki stopped, suddenly furious with herself. She was acting like a coward. If she started falling apart at the beginning of the day, she'd be carried out in pieces by the end of it.

Straightening her shoulders, Nikki made a sharp turn and walked to the front of the classroom. She didn't avoid anyone's eye, although she noticed that some of the kids avoided hers.

Somehow she made it to the front of the room and took a desk right in the middle of the first row. It was the last place Nikki wanted to be, but nobody was going to know that if she could help it.

Mrs. Sheedy, the homeroom teacher, hadn't arrived yet, so the class was on its own. Nikki took out the rainbow pen Nancy had given her and began writing her name in the notebooks she'd brought. The noise rose to an earsplitting level, but it didn't bother Nikki at all. Everything was back to normal —for the moment, anyway.

She was still busy with her notebooks when suddenly there was silence. Nikki raised her head.

But this time, nobody was looking at her. They were all staring at the boy standing in the doorway. He was tall, with unusually beautiful deep gray eyes and thick, dark brown hair. Nikki had never seen him before. She was sure she'd remember him if she had. He must be new, she decided, and returned to her notebooks. Any other time she would have studied him a little more closely, but she wasn't on the lookout for romance. And she'd had her fill of staring.

Before the babble of voices and laughter had a chance to pick up once again, Mrs. Sheedy bustled in. Short and sturdy looking, the teacher strode to the front of the room.

"All right, class," the teacher began briskly, "let me take the roll and then we'll get on with business." She consulted her notebook and called out the first name.

"Hi."

Nikki looked up. The new boy had just sat

down in the next seat and was smiling at her.
"Hi," she replied.

"Timothy Cooper?" Mrs. Sheedy said.

"Here," the boy answered, then turned back to Nikki, still smiling. "I was going to introduce myself, but she beat me to it. Most people call me Tim," he added.

Nikki nodded, gave him a quick return smile, and opened her blue spiral notebook.

"I'm new in River Heights," Tim went on in a low voice. "We just moved here from Chicago."

"Christina Martinez?" Mrs. Sheedy continued.

"Here," a girl answered from the back of the room.

"What's your name?" Tim asked.

"Nicola Masters?" the teacher called.

"Here," Nikki replied. "Most people call me Nikki."

Tim laughed quietly. "I guess that answers my question."

Nikki laughed, too, but she couldn't help thinking that it wouldn't be long before Tim heard all the gossip about her. In another half-hour or so, he probably wouldn't have needed to ask her name.

"All right," Mrs. Sheedy said. "On to the announcements. Tryouts for the drama club's production of *Our Town* will be next

Tuesday immediately after last period. Anyone interested should sign up on the sheet next to the auditorium door."

Nikki jotted down a reminder to herself.

"How is the drama club here?" asked Tim, who was also writing down the information. "Any good?"

"Very," Nikki told him. "There's lots of competition for roles."

"Great," Tim said. "I'm really interested in acting, but if I don't get a part, I'll settle for painting scenery. Anything to be part of a show."

Mrs. Sheedy was reading more announcements. "All transfer students should report to the office some time today to get their counselors' names and schedule a meeting with him or her."

Tim wrote down another note and shook his head. "I hope I can find the main office," he said with a chuckle. "I already got lost once this morning."

"Students driving cars to school must have parking permits," Mrs. Sheedy intoned. "If you didn't get one in the mail, please report to the office and get it taken care of."

A slight frown appeared on Tim's face. "I walked today," he whispered to Nikki. "It was a lot farther than I thought, so I'll probably have to start taking the bus. I was pretty impressed—River Heights is a really nice-looking town. Have you lived here long?"

"All my life," Nikki answered distractedly. She knew Tim was probably a little nervous, starting at a new school, but she wished he'd find someone else to talk to. She hoped Tim didn't think she was rude, but she just didn't feel up to making polite conversation.

"Two more announcements," Mrs. Sheedy was saying. "First, regarding lunch."

The class gave a collective groan, but Mrs. Sheedy plowed ahead. "The staff will not be responsible for any items left in the cafeteria."

"No, they'll just be responsible for the food poisoning!" someone quipped. Everyone laughed.

"And second, your locker assignments are permanent," Mrs. Sheedy began. But half a dozen conversations had broken out, and she almost had to shout the rest of the announcement. "No exchanging with anyone. You people!" she added, pointing to the noisiest group of talkers, "I suggest that you pay closer attention in your next class. Junior year is no piece of cake."

"Yeah, it'll be tough all right," Erik Nielson chimed in. "A real killer!"

At the word *killer,* all conversation died. Nikki could feel everyone's eyes on her, practically boring holes in her back.

Tim turned around, looking confused. "What—" he began, raising an eyebrow at Nikki.

But Nikki was already on her feet, her cheeks flaming. She shot Tim one quick, despairing look, then gathered up her notebooks and raced for the door as the first-period bell rang.

Tim checked his class assignment card. Lunch? No, he had one more class before lunch. Honors English. Good. The more he read, the more he'd learn about people, and the better actor he'd be someday. Stuffing the card back in his pocket, he walked on, checking the room numbers. Room 205 . . . 207 . . . Room 209 must be around the corner. He collided just then with someone who was just straightening up from the water fountain.

"So," a soft voice said, "we meet again."

It was the girl Tim had run into outside that morning. Beverly? Bethany?

"Brittany Tate," she said. "Remember me?"

"Sure," Tim replied with a smile. He might have forgotten her name, but she was easy to remember. Dark hair, great eyes, terrific figure. Friendly, too. But she wasn't Nikki Masters. Nikki was the girl who'd really caught his attention.

"Well," Tim said quickly, "at least I didn't knock you over this time."

"Oh, don't worry about that." She swayed toward him so that he caught a faint whiff of flowery perfume. "I'm glad to see you again. How has it been going?"

"Not bad so far," Tim said. "Everyone seems pretty friendly."

"That's good," Brittany said. She moved even closer and touched him lightly on the arm. "So, where are you headed? I'll be glad to help you find your classroom."

"Thanks, but I think I already have," Tim told her. "Two-oh-nine, honors English. Mr. McNeil. Am I heading in the right direction?"

Brittany's lovely mouth broke into a wide smile. "What a coincidence! That's where I'm going, too." Gracefully linking her arm through his, Brittany propelled him toward the room.

Tim saw Nikki the minute they walked inside. That soft blond hair, the pretty blue sweater that matched her eyes. He'd been worried that he'd see her only in homeroom, but here she was. Now all he had to do was figure out a way to sit next to her.

Luck wasn't on his side this time. Mr. McNeil seated his classes in alphabetical order, and Tim wound up on the opposite side of the room from Nikki.

Of course, he didn't know her at all. And she had been kind of cool this morning. He was afraid he'd annoyed her with all his questions. Not that he blamed her; he'd been babbling like an idiot. But he'd never expected that spark he felt the minute he laid eyes on her, and he couldn't seem to stop talking.

She'd smiled at him—only once—but he knew then she wasn't mad at him. He decided Nikki probably had a lot on her mind. Then that weird thing had happened. The place had gotten as silent as a tomb and Nikki jumped up, looking as if she'd been slapped in the face.

Tim had no idea what that was all about. He was curious, but it didn't really matter. What did matter was getting to know Nikki.

"Good morning." Mr. McNeil spoke softly, but the class quieted down immediately. He was young and extremely gawky, but he had a well-earned reputation as one of the toughest—and best—teachers in the school.

"I'm passing out the first semester's reading list," Mr. McNeil went on, handing a stack of papers to a girl in the front row. "Look it over and then we'll talk about the first book, *The Scarlet Letter*. I want you to read the first fifty pages by Thursday. The library has only three copies, but the bookstore has plenty—I checked. If anyone has trouble finding the book or can't afford a copy, please talk to me. I've got a few copies stashed away at home."

He looked around the class and smiled. "Do any of you know the story?" he asked. Most of the hands shot up. "So, let's talk. What is it about Hester Prynne that has kept Hawthorne's book alive all these years?"

Somebody mentioned loneliness, someone else suggested courage, and then Ellen Ming, the junior class treasurer, mentioned ostracism.

"Hester was shut out," she said. "Everybody can sympathize with her because everybody knows that feeling. You know. Like Nikki." Then her face flushed. "Oh, I'm sorry, Nikki. I wasn't thinking."

Everyone stared in Nikki's direction. She looked at the floor.

Mr. McNeil cleared his throat. "That's an interesting point, Ellen, but I think we should have Nikki's okay before we discuss it any further."

Nikki raised her eyes, started to shake her head, then shrugged and nodded.

Tim was shocked at the discussion that followed. How Nikki's boyfriend had been killed, how Nikki was accused of murder.

How, until Nancy Drew had stepped in and solved the crime, almost everybody had believed that Nikki *had* killed Dan Taylor.

The discussion was still going on when the bell rang. Shoulders back, eyes looking straight ahead, Nikki was the first one out the door.

Tim watched her leave, gazing intently after her.

Her own eyes narrowed to slits, Brittany watched Tim watch Nikki. It was impossible to tell what he was thinking just then. Earlier, when class had started, she'd known *exactly* what he was thinking. And that had been maddening.

Tim hadn't taken his eyes off Nikki for one second. Just her luck, Brittany thought miserably. There were two honors English classes, and Nikki Masters had to be in the same one as Tim Cooper. And without lifting a finger, Nikki had Tim looking at her as if she were the only girl in the world.

That was what really burned Brittany. Nikki Masters never had to try for anything.

For the first ten minutes of class, Brittany had felt like screaming. But then, thanks to Ellen Ming putting her foot in her mouth, things had brightened up. Nikki's whole awful story had come tumbling out, and Tim had heard it. Maybe now he wouldn't get so interested in her.

Of course, she didn't know how Tim felt. But she knew how she felt. She was crazy about him. She wanted him for herself. And she was going to get him.

3 ～～

"What happened to Lacey?" Nikki asked as she and Robin joined the cafeteria line. "I thought she was going to eat with us."

"Rick Stratton happened to Lacey." Robin rolled her eyes. "Have you seen him? He went from nerd to hunk in one summer. He spent all of vacation climbing in the Rockies. Lacey told him *she* was really interested in climbing, too. So now they're walking around outside, talking about the joys of nature."

"Lacey?" Nikki shook her head in disbelief. "When did Lacey discover the great outdoors?"

"When she discovered the new Rick Stratton, of course," Robin replied. "If things get going between them, Lacey'll have to take a crash course in fitness.''

Nikki laughed.

"Well, at least you can laugh. When I met you in the hall a few minutes ago, your chin was practically dragging on the floor," Robin said bluntly.

"Are my feelings that obvious?" Nikki asked.

"Not to everyone," Robin answered. She took a tray for herself and handed one to Nikki. "But I noticed. Have things been that bad?"

"Pretty bad," Nikki said quietly. Then she filled Robin in on the embarrassing incidents in homeroom and English.

"Jeez!" Robin said indignantly. "How could Mr. McNeil let them talk about you like that?"

"He didn't," Nikki said, reaching for a salad platter. "He asked me if it was all right. I started to say no, but then I changed my mind and said yes."

"You did?" Robin's big eyes widened. "Why?"

"Oh, I guess because everybody's talking about me, anyway," Nikki replied. "So I just figured, why not let them do it to my face?"

"That took guts," Robin said admiringly. "But I bet you were right. Maybe now everybody'll shut up."

Nikki hoped so, but she had her doubts. She could see several people staring at her right then and there in the cafeteria.

That new guy, for instance: Tim Cooper. There he was with Brittany Tate, over at a table by the window. Brittany was sitting as close to him as she could possibly get without being in his lap, but Tim didn't seem to notice. He was looking at Nikki. Or at least he had been, until he'd met her eyes. Then he'd looked away.

"Hey," Robin said, lowering her voice. "Do you see that guy Brittany's drooling over? He must be the terrific new transfer student I keep hearing about."

"He is," Nikki said. "His name is Tim Cooper. He's from Chicago—I think." He'd said a lot of things, she suddenly remembered, but she hadn't been paying much attention.

"Well, I can see why everyone's talking about him," Robin said. "He's definitely gorgeous." She took a carton of milk and a bunch of napkins. "Speaking of gorgeous," she went on, her voice casual, "what do you think of Calvin Roth?"

"Calvin Roth?" Nikki tried to place him. Light brown hair, green eyes, dimples. "Very cute," she told Robin. "Very smart, too, I hear."

"Yeah, a real wizard. Especially in

science. He's my lab partner in chemistry," Robin said.

"And you're interested!" Nikki cried. "That's great, Robin. I take it the interest's mutual?"

"I don't know yet." Robin looked uncomfortable. "I hope so. I mean, there was definitely some chemistry going on, but . . ." She faltered to a stop and blushed. Robin *never* blushed.

"Come on, Robin, out with it," Nikki demanded.

Robin lowered her voice until she was practically whispering. "He's—uh—he's an inch shorter than I am."

"So what?" Nikki couldn't help laughing. "That doesn't matter, and you know it. For your information, I think you and Calvin are a perfect match. As long as you don't wear heels," she added teasingly.

"Very funny," Robin said. "Anyway, we'll just wait and see." She handed her lunch ticket to the cashier and glanced around the cafeteria. "Something's happening over there by the window, that's for sure," she said. "Brittany's working pretty fast. She might as well hang a sign around that new guy's neck, saying 'Mine'!"

Yes, Brittany was definitely after Tim Cooper, Nikki thought with a wry smile. That had been obvious the minute Nikki had seen them come into class together. She didn't know how Tim felt, but Brittany had a reputation for getting what she wanted.

If things had been different, Nikki might have been interested in Tim herself. He was the best-looking guy she'd ever seen, and he also seemed genuinely nice.

"Come on," Robin said as they left the line. "There's a table over there that isn't too crowded."

As Nikki followed Robin through the maze of tables and chairs, she knew she was being stared at again. She reminded herself to ignore the strange glances, but it was hard.

As they neared the table that Robin had pointed out, the three girls sitting there scooted their chairs over to make room for them. *Way* over, Nikki noticed. Clear to the far end. Now half a table separated them from the notorious Nikki Masters.

Nikki sat down and peeled back the foil lid on her salad dressing. Her hands were shaking. It was ridiculous to be so upset, but she couldn't help it. "Don't say anything, Robin," she said softly. "Please."

Robin took a bit of her tuna sandwich. "Why not?" she asked, chewing furiously.

"Because you're not going to stop the gossip," Nikki said. "Look around. I'm the hottest topic of conversation here. And it's not just those three girls. It's the entire student body of River Heights High!"

As if to prove her point, a bleached-blond, denim-clad girl walked past their table with her boyfriend, who was clad in black leather and denim. The girl glanced at Nikki, then stopped dead in her tracks, her eyes widening with recognition. "That's her!" she said to the boy. "That's Nikki Masters. She's the one I was telling you about!"

She hadn't even bothered to lower her voice, and everyone had heard her. The cafeteria suddenly grew much quieter.

Even Robin was speechless.

Nikki looked up, fighting the tears that threatened to spill down her cheeks. People were never going to forget.

On the other side of the cafeteria, Brittany looked from Tim to Nikki, then back to Tim again. Her heart sank like a stone. She could read his face like a book. And she didn't like the words at all.

She could see that Tim was disgusted, outraged, appalled—but not with Nikki. No, for Nikki he had only sympathy. It was everybody else who was making him angry. Everybody who was staring at poor little Nikki Masters.

Thank goodness *she* hadn't said anything

negative about Nikki, Brittany thought. Tim had no idea how she felt about the girl, and she planned to keep him in the dark on that.

Should she say something to him about how unfair all the gossip was? Could she manage to keep the words from sticking in her throat? But, no, then she and Tim would be sympathizing together, and the focus would still be on Nikki. She had to do something to get Tim's attention back where she wanted it—on her.

Brittany thought hard and fast. Suddenly she knew exactly what to do. In one quick, fluid motion, she scraped back her chair and rose to her feet. The cafeteria was still quiet, and the sound of her chair caught everyone's attention. All eyes turned to her, just as she'd planned.

Brittany looked out over the crowded room, her dark eyes moving from face to face. The moment was hers, and she was going to make the most of it.

"In case anyone doesn't know," she announced, her sultry voice carrying to the farthest corners of the room, "I write the 'Off the Record' column for the school paper. People tell me it's the most popular column in the *Record,* and I don't mind admitting that I love to hear them say it."

Many of the students nodded. "Off the

Record" was not only popular, it was powerful. Attitudes, fashion, music—they could be raised to the heights of popularity or banished to the depths of oblivion with a stroke of Brittany's pencil.

"But I also have to admit," she went on, giving a modest little laugh, "that sometimes I run out of ideas on what to write about. So I thought this might be a good time to ask everyone to help me out and send me suggestions for future columns."

A few people smiled, but most of them seemed a little puzzled.

"But before you send anything, I'll tell you one thing that's definitely *out,*" Brittany went on. She let her eyes sweep around the room, and when she got to the bleached-blond girl, she paused and looked straight at her. Everyone followed her gaze.

Then Brittany said dramatically, "Stale news is out. Mean gossip is out. Whispering and giggling about innocent people is out." She finally took her eyes off the girl and addressed the crowd again. " 'Off the Record' is about what's hot. The past is out."

Brittany took a deep breath, smiled beautifully, and sat down.

The message had been sent—and received. If you wanted to be "in," you'd better stop talking about Nikki Masters.

Suddenly a cloud of guilt seemed to settle over the room. Students murmured and nodded their heads. Everyone seemed to agree that Nikki had been treated unfairly. The girls at the end of her table smiled shyly and scooted their chairs back.

Nikki felt a tap on her shoulder. Turning, she saw that it was the blond girl whose outburst had started the whole incident.

Nervously fingering her spiky hair, the girl said, "I just want to tell you that I'm sorry for—well, you know—my big mouth. I was really thoughtless, you know?"

"Thanks," Nikki said. "You weren't the only one."

The girl left, and Nikki turned back to Robin. "Incredible!" she said, amazed. "Two minutes ago I was a juicy topic, and now I'm stale news. I won't complain, though. That's exactly what I want."

"It is great," Robin agreed thoughtfully. "But I wonder what got into Brittany. She's not exactly famous for standing up for people."

"I was thinking of that, too," Nikki said. "She must have had *some* reason for doing it—besides helping me, I mean. But it doesn't really matter." She stood up slowly. "Look! I got out of my chair and not a single person noticed. It's over!"

"I get the point," Robin said dryly. "So why don't you sit back down and eat?"

"No time," Nikki told her. "Lunch period is almost over, and I want to catch Brittany before she leaves. She might have had an ulterior motive, but she still helped me. I've got to thank her."

Nikki walked across the cafeteria to Brittany's table. Tim had gone, she noticed, and she felt a little disappointed. This would have been a good time to talk to him for a minute and show him she wasn't as aloof as she had acted that morning.

Brittany now was sitting with Cheryl Worth, the president of the Student Council, and Chris Martinez, the captain of the cheerleading squad. Both of them had ignored Nikki earlier, but now they greeted her as if they were her dearest friends. She smiled to herself. Brittany sure had those two under her thumb.

Nikki smiled. "Thanks, Brittany," she said. "It was great of you to stand up for me like that."

Brittany waved her hand and shrugged modestly. "I'm glad I could help," she said, which wasn't a complete lie. Tim had already left the table, but before he excused himself, he'd given her a thousand-watt smile with those gorgeous gray eyes, and he'd actually put his hand on her shoulder for one brief, delicious moment. Brittany had helped, all right. She'd helped Nikki *and* herself.

"I only said the obvious," Brittany added. "When people are down, they need support."

"Well," Nikki said, "I've got to go. But thanks again, Brittany. I really appreciate it."

Nikki walked back through the cafeteria toward the door. Some people smiled, and a few of them called out greetings. But none of them actually stopped what they were doing and stared or whispered behind their hands. Not a single eyebrow was raised as she passed.

Everything's back to normal, Nikki thought happily. Now my junior year can really begin!

4

"Okay, Brittany, out with it," Kim Bishop demanded. "Why did you stand up for Nikki like that?"

"Yes," Samantha drawled. "We both know you can't stand the girl—you tell us that every chance you get. If I didn't know any better, I'd think you had a change of heart. But," she said with a shrewd smile, "I *do* know better. So, what were you thinking of?"

It was shortly after the final bell, and the three girls were standing by Brittany's locker. Kids were streaming past. Brittany sorted her books and checked her appearance in the mirror taped to the inside of her locker door.

Then she tossed her hair, closed and locked the door, and finally swung around to face her friends.

Smiling, she replied, "Don't you two know that you bait a trap with honey, not with vinegar?"

Kim looked puzzled, but Samantha's eyes lit up instantly.

"Aha!" she said, turning to Kim. "That's Brittany's subtle way of saying she's after a boy."

Brittany laughed. She and Samantha almost always thought alike. "You've got it," she answered. "But I bet you don't know who he is."

"You're going to tell us, aren't you?" Kim asked.

"I'll give you a hint," Brittany teased. "Deep gray eyes, gorgeous dark hair, a build to die for? You told me about him this morning, remember?"

Kim's brows shot up. "That actor? Tom Something?"

"Tim," Brittany corrected. "Tim Cooper."

"Right, from Chicago," Kim said. "Well, I finally saw him, and all I can say is, you've got good taste, Brittany."

"My, my, you sure do!" Samantha chuckled. "And just think, I was all set to go after him myself."

"Too late," Brittany told her, grinning.

"Oh, well," Samantha said, sighing heavily.

Brittany knew Samantha wasn't the least bit heartbroken. Chasing boys was only a sport for her. Finding them and going after them was the fun part. Once she caught one, she quickly lost interest.

"But what does all this have to do with your standing up for Nikki?" Kim asked.

With a smug sense of satisfaction, Brittany related the cafeteria incident. "Of course, I didn't enjoy turning things around for Nikki," she added when she finished. "But it was worth it when Tim gave me that terrific smile."

Kim nodded approvingly, and Samantha shook her head. "You sure do work fast, Brittany," she said. "Why, you even put me to shame."

Laughing together, the three girls started down the hall. Brittany felt wonderful. In fact, she was on top of the world.

Ten seconds later she was at the bottom again. They had just started down the hall that led past the auditorium when Brittany stopped suddenly.

There, signing a sheet that was posted next to the auditorium door, was Tim Cooper. Right next to him was Nikki Masters.

"Uh-oh," Samantha said under her breath.

"'Uh-oh' is right," Kim agreed. "He'll never put his name on that list if he doesn't take his eyes off Nikki."

Immediately Brittany slid around a corner out of sight, Kim and Samantha hot on her heels.

Tim was still interested in Nikki! Brittany's kind, generous, thoughtful gesture in the cafeteria had been completely wasted! Why had she even bothered to open her mouth?

Brittany wanted to scream, but she couldn't let anyone see how upset she was. Not even Kim and Samantha. She didn't want them to know how hard she'd fallen for Tim. They'd probably think she was crazy and might even laugh at her.

She took a deep breath and forced herself to smile. "A minor setback, that's all," she said, keeping her tone light.

"It looked like a pretty major setback to me," Kim remarked.

"Who cares?" Samantha laughed gleefully. "This makes the whole game much more interesting. Why, it wouldn't be any fun at all if there wasn't a challenge! Right, Brittany?"

Brittany had pulled herself together. "Right," she agreed without batting an eyelash.

"Well, come on, then," Samantha urged.

"Let's get going. We can discuss your strategy on the way home."

The three of them lived in the same neighborhood and usually rode home together, but Brittany couldn't face the bus ride now. She needed to be alone so she could do some serious thinking.

"You two go on," she said quickly. "DeeDee keeps bugging me about that deadline, so I think I'll walk home. I can work out the column on the way."

Outside, Brittany waved goodbye to Kim and Samantha and slowly headed home. Walking was better than taking the bus, anyway. She hated the bus. Of course, a car would be best, but how was she going to convince her father of that? "The bus gets you to school just as fast," he liked to say. He didn't understand that a car was more than a means of transportation.

She wondered briefly if Tim had a car. Probably. A guy like that somehow didn't belong on a bus. But she and Nikki had something in common besides Tim Cooper. Nikki didn't have a car, which was another thing that drove Brittany crazy. Nikki had been born with a silver spoon in her mouth; she could probably have anything she wanted merely by asking. Why she rode a tacky school bus was beyond Brittany's comprehension. If *she* had Nikki's money, she'd be behind the wheel of a Porsche this very minute.

Leaving the school grounds, Brittany turned west. It wasn't the shortest route home, but it took her through the nicest neighborhood in River Heights—the one in which she longed to live. It was an area of broad streets lined with maple trees, sweeping lawns, and large houses for the city's oldest and wealthiest families.

Soon Brittany came to Nikki Masters's house, and next to it, Nancy Drew's. Both were lovely homes—Nikki's was an elegant Tudor-style with quaint casement windows —but they were by no means the grandest in the area. The largest houses lay a couple of blocks west on a wide avenue divided by a beautifully landscaped median. The largest mansion of all, which looked like a French château, sat amid acres of perfect green lawn, surrounded by a towering wrought-iron fence.

When she drew near that house, Brittany stood in the shade of a massive oak tree and looked longingly through the fence. The Masters mansion was stunning—and to think that Nikki's grandfather, Philip Masters, lived there all by himself!

Built-in sprinklers threw water in wide arcs across the lawn. To one side of the house, Brittany could see two clay tennis courts and a manicured croquet pitch. Behind the house, she had heard, was an enormous swimming pool. Beyond that lay woods, and beyond the woods lay the green fairways of the River Heights Country Club, founded by Nikki's great-grandfather.

Brittany yearned with all her heart to be part of that gracious, privileged world, but she wasn't. Her family was boringly ordinary. Instead of founding an industrial empire, her own great-grandfather had managed an ice company that went bankrupt when electric refrigerators were invented. Instead of owning Masters Electronics, her father merely worked there.

Giving herself a little shake, Brittany finally turned away from the Masters home. Twenty minutes later she reached her own neighborhood. The houses—either ranches or split levels—were roomy and well cared for, with good-size yards, thriving young trees, and two-car garages. It was a nice enough neighborhood, she admitted. But it couldn't hold a candle to the one she'd just left.

As she walked up the driveway to her house, a cedar-shingled ranch, her spirits picked up a bit. One of the garage doors was open, and she could see her father inside. Even though he wasn't a millionaire, Brittany did love him very much.

"What are you doing here?" she asked, dropping her books on the hood of her mother's Dodge Colt.

"The boss gave me the afternoon off," James Tate explained with a grin. "'Key employees need to relax every now and then,' he said."

Brittany winced. She was glad that her dad was so valuable to Masters Electronics, but she hated it when he referred to Nikki's father as "the boss." It was true, but she didn't like being reminded of it, especially now.

She watched her dad work, smiling for the first time since she'd left school. He was repairing their vacuum cleaner, the same ancient, bubble-shaped monster they'd had her whole life. It roared like a sick water buffalo and broke down once a month, but Mr. Tate refused to replace it. "Why pay for new when used works just as well?" he liked to say.

It made him sound cheap, Brittany knew, but he wasn't. He just loved to fix things.

"So how was school?" he asked, unscrewing the vacuum pump from its housing.

"Okay. Same as last year," Brittany answered.

"I didn't hear the bus," he said. "Did you get a ride home?"

"No, I walked." Brittany sighed out loud.

"I thought you enjoyed walking home."

"Now, but not in winter," she replied.

"No, I guess not."

"But if I had a car . . ." Brittany hesitated.

Her dad smiled without looking up. "That tune sounds familiar. Where have I heard it before?"

Brittany swallowed. "Come on, Dad, we can afford a third car, can't we?"

"Yes, we can afford one," he told her. "But the problem is, Brittany, a car is a headache. I doubt you'd want all that responsibility."

"Try me!"

Mr. Tate looked up. He was a tall man, with kind brown eyes, brown hair, and a hairline that he jokingly claimed was a victim of "beach erosion."

He smiled at Brittany. "I'll think about it," he said.

Brittany felt her shoulders slump. He'd said that before. She'd just have to wait awhile and try again.

With another sigh, she scooped up her books. Her father was bent over his workbench once again, whistling happily. She couldn't help feeling glad to see him so relaxed. The pressures at work had been pretty intense lately. Mr. Tate had designed an important new product—a simple motor control that allowed big electric motors to do the same work using twenty percent less energy—and the problems of getting it onto the market were taking their toll on him.

Brittany kissed her father on the cheek and went inside. Her mother and little sister, Tamara, weren't around. Mrs. Tate often worked late at her florist's shop in the mall. Dinner was all ready, though. She peeked into the oven and groaned. A casserole! Ugh. Tamara had probably made it.

Brittany hurried to her room and shut the door. At least there she had things the way she wanted them. Her bed was a canopied four-poster, trimmed with a dainty print fabric, and the wallpaper was striped. Knick-knacks adorned her dresser, and an oval mirror hung above it. The room almost, but not quite, duplicated her favorite bedroom in *Town and Country* magazine.

Tossing her books on the desk, Brittany flopped down on her bed with the latest copy of *Vogue* and began leafing through it rapidly, annoyed at herself.

She had completely wasted the walk home. She still had no idea what she was going to do about Tim Cooper, but she would come up with something. She had to. If she had Tim, her life would be every bit as magical as she wanted it to be.

She wanted *him.* Now all she had to do was get him to want her.

Tossing the magazine aside, Brittany sat up, her teeth clenched. One thing was certain: there was no way she would let Nikki Masters walk off with Tim Cooper. If she had to fight for him, then so be it. She'd fight— and win.

5 ～～～

The next day, dressed in her softest pair of stone-washed jeans, an oversize, buttercup yellow top, and well-worn sneakers, Nikki fitted the zoom lens onto her camera and got ready to take one final shot. She'd have to hurry to get to homeroom on time, but this last picture would definitely be worth it.

On the other side of the quad stood Lacey and the new, well-built Rick Stratton. Lacey had bent Nikki's ear about the guy during the bus ride that morning. The girl was so head-over-heels in love that she was actually talking about taking up some form of outdoor exercise.

Carefully, Nikki focused and took the shot. If DeeDee Smith didn't use it in the

Record, at least Lacey would have a picture of herself and the new guy in her life.

Nikki glanced at her watch. No time for any more pictures now. She unscrewed the lens and put everything away in her leather camera bag. Then she slung the heavy bag over one shoulder and her purse over the other, grabbed her books up from the lawn, and hurried toward the school building.

DeeDee, the pretty black editor with the serious eyes, caught up to Nikki just as she was going through the door. "How did you do?" she asked. "Did you get some good shots?"

"I'm pretty sure I did," Nikki replied. "I got a really good wide-angle photo of the quad. It should be perfect for a two-page spread."

"Great, and thanks, Nikki. If it comes out, I'll use it as the first-day photo in the *Record.*" She laughed. "Of course, this *is* the second day, but we can fake it. There's not much difference, anyway."

Not for you, maybe, Nikki thought, waving goodbye to DeeDee and heading for 101 North. For her, there was a world of difference between the two days. Gone were the sidelong glances, the not-so-quiet whispers, the gawking and staring.

"Need any help?" a voice asked as Nikki reached the door of her homeroom.

Turning, she saw Tim Cooper right behind her. The weather was still gloriously warm, and Tim had on a teal blue polo shirt that did wonders for his eyes.

"Thanks," she answered with a laugh, "but I have to get used to carrying all this stuff. Most photographers can't afford to hire someone to carry their bags."

Nikki and Tim entered homeroom together and headed for their desks in the front row.

"Is that what you want to be?" Tim asked as they sat down. "A photographer?"

"Oh, I don't know, really," Nikki replied. "What about you? Are you serious about acting?"

She had run into Tim outside the auditorium the day before, when they were both signing up for the *Our Town* auditions. But she'd been in a hurry and hadn't had time to talk. Now, since Mrs. Sheedy was late again, they would have a few minutes, at least.

"So far I'm serious," Tim said. "I was lucky to get some walk-ons in Chicago, and I danced in a few commercials, too. But it's a tough profession—and I've got a long way to go."

At least he's realistic, Nikki thought. Then she remembered what he'd said about painting scenery just to be a part of the production. So he really must love the theater. She smiled.

Tim smiled back, and Nikki was hit again by how great-looking he was. She felt a blush start to creep up her face. This wasn't what she wanted, she told herself firmly. She wasn't ready to be attracted to *any* guy, no matter how open and down-to-earth and handsome he was.

Slightly flustered, she cleared her throat. "Well, I hope you make it," she said. "Maybe someday you'll be a famous graduate of River Heights High."

"Thanks," Tim answered with an easy laugh. "But right now I'd just be happy for any part in *Our Town*. Speaking of famous," he went on, "I noticed a huge industrial park out by the interstate. The sign said it was all part of Masters Electronics." He grinned. "I bet everyone asks if your family owns the company, right?"

"Actually, ownership is split between my granddad, my dad, and me," Nikki told him. "But I don't get to vote my shares yet. I'm supposed to graduate from college first."

Tim stared at her in astonishment. "You're not kidding, are you?" he asked.

Nikki shook her head. "I thought you knew, or at least had guessed," she said. "I mean, you heard the whole story of my life yesterday, didn't you?"

Tim was looking straight at her, his eyes warm and caring. "I heard a lot about you yesterday," he admitted. "But all that was just one part of your life." He ran a hand through his thick hair and smiled, looking a little nervous. "I'd like to know more about you," he said. "The good parts *and* the bad."

The blush was coming back—Nikki could feel it. She leaned her elbows on the desk and cupped her chin in her hands, hoping to hide it. "There's a lot more good than bad," she said after clearing her throat again. "But that was definitely the worst."

Tim nodded. "It sounded pretty bad," he said. "And yesterday must have been terrible for you, at least until lunch."

Nikki looked down at her desk.

"You know," Tim went on thoughtfully, "yesterday I felt as if I understood part of what you were going through. As if we had something in common."

Nikki looked at him questioningly.

"Because I'm new here," he explained quickly. "I mean, the new kid in school always gets talked about, right? It's embarrassing. I was expecting it to happen," he added, "but that didn't make my first day any easier. I wish it were about three months from now. That way, I'd already have friends and know my way around."

Almost without thinking, Nikki said, "Well, I can help you with that. I've lived here all my life. I'd be glad to show you around if you'd like. And I have some great friends, too."

Tim laughed and shook his head. "I didn't mean to sound as if I was feeling sorry for myself," he said.

"I know you weren't," Nikki told him. "Really, it would be fun."

"Well, thanks!" Tim looked pleased. "And listen, I meant what I said about getting to know you. I'd really like to talk to you more—a lot more."

Just then Mrs. Sheedy entered the room, looking harried and out of breath. Immediately she began reading the announcements at top speed.

Nikki barely heard her. Her feelings were completely mixed up. What had she just gotten herself into?

Sneaking a look at Tim's ruggedly handsome profile, she had to admit to herself that she was attracted to him. Be honest, Nikki, she told herself, you're more than just attracted. Something special might even happen if you let it.

But, no, she wasn't going to allow herself to become involved with anyone. Not after her disastrous experience with Dan. She'd let something special happen with him, and it had been the biggest mistake of her life. She wasn't going to make another one, not with someone she hardly knew.

And what about Tim? she thought, watching his strong-looking hand as he took notes. Okay, so he was handsome, warm, and friendly. But was he too friendly? He had said he wanted to be an actor. Maybe all that talk about wanting to get to know her was just acting. Maybe he figured that one day he'd play the part of a person accused of a terrible crime, and she'd be able to give him some pointers on what it felt like. He'd seemed sincere, but was he?

One voice told Nikki that she was being ridiculous. Another voice told her to be careful. She decided to listen to the second one—not because she didn't trust Tim, but because she couldn't trust herself.

Brittany cruised down the hall, feeling desperate. Nobody could tell, of course. She'd mastered the trick of hiding her emotions, and besides, she knew she looked good. She was wearing a black leather miniskirt—bought on sale—black stockings, black flats, and a long gray suit jacket. Just the thing to appeal to a sophisticated guy from Chicago, she hoped. Now all she had to do was find him.

That was why she was so desperate. She hadn't seen Tim since English, and he wasn't in the cafeteria at lunch.

Lunch was over now, and if she didn't find

him soon, she might not see him again until the next day. Brittany could hardly believe she was going this crazy over a guy.

The only bright spot was that Nikki didn't seem to be interested in Tim. When English was over, she'd just given him a neutral smile and hurried out of the room.

But Brittany had no doubt how Tim felt about Nikki. Somehow she had to get him to pay attention to *her*. But how could she, if she couldn't even find him?

Finally! There he was, at his locker. Curving her lips into her most winning smile, Brittany zoomed off in his direction.

As she approached Tim, she noticed that he was reading a letter. The paper was pale pink. Was it from a girlfriend? she wondered, her heart suddenly sinking. No, if he had a girlfriend back in Chicago, he wouldn't be interested in Nikki.

Perking up, she called out, "Tim, hi!"

"Oh, hi, Brittany," he answered, hastily folding the letter and tucking it into one of the books he was carrying. He smiled at her. "Hey, nice outfit."

Brittany felt like melting. She also felt a quiver of hope. At least he wasn't completely blinded by Nikki's charms.

"Thank you," she said, giving him a modest smile. Then she quickly changed the subject. It wasn't that she didn't love being the focal point of the conversation, but she didn't want Tim to think she was conceited. "That's quite a pile of books," she commented. "Don't tell me you're already starting on a term paper."

Tim shook his head. "No, this was just some background reading I did on Hawthorne last night. I'm really enjoying English, aren't you?"

"Oh, yes!" Brittany agreed enthusiastically. So the guy was brainy, too. Good, she was also bright. Of course, with all the clubs she belonged to, she usually had to play catch-up with her schoolwork, but she always managed to get good grades.

"Actually, I was just about to take them back to the library," he said, closing his locker.

"That's exactly where I was headed," Brittany lied. So what? She had study hall next, anyway, and she could always do her homework that night. Tim must have study hall now, too. Too bad they weren't in the same one.

"Why don't you walk there with me?" Tim said casually.

"I'd be glad to," Brittany said, trying to ignore the fact that her stomach was starting to flip over again. This couldn't have gone better if she'd planned it.

As they made their way to the library, Brittany carefully considered her approach. She wanted Tim to like her, but she knew she couldn't come on too strong.

"I was hoping to see you at lunch today," she told him.

"I had to miss it to meet with my counselor," Tim replied. "Can't you hear my stomach growling?"

"No, not really," Brittany said, giggling. "I heard you're interested in acting. It's such a glamorous occupation. I'm really fascinated."

"So am I," he said with a wry chuckle. "But after doing a couple of commercials, I found out that it's about one percent glamour and ninety-nine percent sweat."

Brittany tried not to let her mouth drop open. *Commercials!* He'd actually made commercials! But if Tim was going to be so modest and blasé about it, then she would be, too. She'd act any way he wanted her to.

Brittany tried to think of something else to say. Why wasn't *he* talking more? After all, he'd invited her to walk with him, right? He must have wanted her company. Or was he just being nice, the way he would be to any friend?

Brittany shuddered at the thought of being considered just "any" friend. But when they reached the library, Tim opened the door for her, and Brittany's heart soared as heads turned in their direction. It would all be perfect if only she didn't feel that Tim had simply been making polite conversation with her.

"Well, thanks for walking with me," he said, heading for the main desk. "I've got to get back to study hall and try to make sense out of my chem book. I guess I'll see you tomorrow in English."

Rats, Brittany thought. Now I'm stuck in the library. "Okay," she said cheerfully. "And by the way, I'd be more than happy to show you around town if you'd like."

"That's nice, Brittany," Tim said, "but I already made plans to take the grand tour with Nikki Masters. Thanks for the offer, though." Hurriedly depositing his books on the return cart, Tim flashed her another quick smile and walked out of the library.

Stunned, Brittany stood by the cart. Nikki Masters had already offered? Naturally. Even if Nikki wasn't interested in Tim, she'd be nice to him. Nikki was always nice—not disgustingly sweet, Brittany had to admit—but plain, simple, down-to-earth nice. A decent human being, in fact.

Well, Brittany would be like that, too, someday. When she could afford to be.

In the meantime, what was she going to do about Tim Cooper? Stumped, Brittany stared at the books Tim had left on the cart as if they might contain the answer.

They didn't, but one of them contained something else—Tim's letter. He'd forgotten it.

Brittany took the pink sheet out of the book, and a small photograph fluttered to the floor. She picked it up and stared at the girl in the picture. She was standing with her back to the camera, looking over her shoulder. She had pouty lips and a wild mane of blond hair, and she wore a skimpy skirt that fit like a second skin, with a sweater cut low in the back. Scrawled on the back of the picture were the words, "Love you still. Yvette."

Sexy, Brittany thought, but hardly subtle. After a swift, furtive glance around the library, Brittany slipped Tim's letter and the picture into her purse. Then she tore a sheet of paper from her notebook, folded it, and walked up to the main desk.

She put the Hawthorne book back on the cart, then held up the piece of paper. "I found this in one of the books," she said to the librarian. "I'm not sure what to do with it. It's only got a couple of words scribbled on it." That was true. It was a two-item shopping list—panty hose and eyeliner.

"Let me see." The librarian took the note, scanned it, and just as Brittany had hoped, deposited it in the wastebasket.

On her way out of the library, Brittany held the door open for the janitor and his utility cart. The man was on his way in to do his twice-daily emptying of the wastebaskets. Perfect! If Tim came back looking for the letter, the librarian would tell him that it had been taken to the incinerator.

Now for the letter! Leaning against a bank of lockers, Brittany removed the letter from her purse. Then she opened her spiral notebook and carefully concealed the letter and photograph inside.

She took a quick glance at the end. "Your pal, Lonnie." Lonnie? Brittany had thought the letter was from Yvette. Frowning, she started at the beginning.

Dear Tim,

So how are things in River Heights? Are you getting bored yet? After Chicago, how could you not?

We all really miss you, especially Yvette!! She asked me to send you this picture so you wouldn't forget her. As if any male over the age of ten could possibly forget Yvette Weiss!!! I'll bet River Heights doesn't have anybody like *her*, does it?

The rest of the letter mentioned other friends, Tim's old school, dull stuff like that. The only good thing was the part about Yvette.

So, Brittany thought, putting the note back in her purse, Tim goes for girls like Yvette Weiss. Very interesting. Then why did he seem to like Nikki so much? Was it her blond hair? Yvette had blond hair, too.

Brittany's hair was dark, but she could start dressing like Yvette. She had to use this information.

When the bell rang, the hall quickly filled with students. Brittany was so deep in thought as she headed toward her next class that she almost bumped into the two girls in front of her. When she realized who they were—Nikki and her friend, Spacey Lacey —she moved closer and listened to their conversation.

"Today, right after school," Nikki was saying. "A real shop-till-you-drop invasion of the mall."

"I'd love to go shopping," Lacey said. "And I would if I weren't going for a walk with Rick."

Lacey said something else, but Brittany missed it. She strained her ears to catch Nikki's response.

"Well, Robin's got swim practice, so I guess I'll have to go alone," Nikki said. "I'm sick of everything I've got. It's time for a whole new wardrobe."

The two girls turned the corner, but Brittany didn't bother to follow them. She stood in the hall, students rushing past her, and smiled to herself.

Now she really knew what to do with that letter. And if her plan worked out, Tim Cooper was as good as hers.

6

The mall was jammed. It seemed as if just about every girl—and half the guys—in River Heights had picked that afternoon to shop for a fall wardrobe. Nikki loved the whole bustling atmosphere.

"There's just one problem," she said. "I'm not sure it's possible to get near a single store."

Brittany Tate laughed. "Sure it is! Think like a snowplow!" Still laughing, she linked elbows with Nikki and pulled her past the fountain at the mall's entrance and into the thick of the crowd.

Nikki was surprised to find herself shopping with Brittany. When she'd run into Brittany outside the mall and thanked her again for coming to her defense the day before, Brittany had suggested that they shop together, and Nikki couldn't come up with a reason not to.

"Glad Rags," Nikki said now, pointing toward a boutique featuring the latest fashions. "That's the place I want to go first. They've got great stuff."

"I love it, too," Brittany said, smiling enthusiastically. "Let's buy out the store!"

Glad Rags was a trendy high-tech shop, with flashing lights, lots of mirrors, and rock music pulsating from hidden speakers.

"Oh, look at that!" Brittany gasped, dropping Nikki's arm and drifting over to a mannequin wearing a black minidress. "Isn't it *great?*" She turned and narrowed her eyes, giving Nikki a critical look. "You know, this dress would really show off your blond hair."

"That, and a whole lot more," Nikki joked, inspecting the dress. "I'm not sure where I'd wear it, but you're right. It's fantastic."

"Then don't worry about where you'd wear it," Brittany said. "If you like it, go for it!"

Nikki laughed, enjoying Brittany's gutsy, positive attitude. "Well, let's look around a bit first."

The girls began to wander among the racks, quickly flicking through their contents. "I haven't been shopping in ages," Nikki said after a while. "It feels great."

"I bet it does," Brittany agreed. "I mean, after what you went through this summer, you must feel like a different person."

"That's it!" Nikki was surprised but pleased that Brittany understood what she was talking about. "That's exactly how I feel."

Brittany smiled, and then her dark eyes grew thoughtful. "You know, Nikki," she said hesitantly, "I've been feeling kind of bad about things. I mean, there you were, going through such an awful time this summer, and I"—she shook her head and lowered her eyes—"I should have called you, at least. I want you to know I'm sorry I didn't."

"Thanks, Brittany," Nikki said. People sure were unpredictable, she thought. She would never have expected Brittany to apologize. "You weren't the only one who didn't call me," Nikki said. "And, anyway," she went on with a laugh, "you more than made up for it at lunch yesterday."

"Well, I hope so," Brittany said. "It just made me furious, everybody whispering and staring like a bunch of idiots." She shivered. "If it had been *me* they were staring at like that, I would have died!"

"Well, it's over now," Nikki said, laughing again. "And since I feel like a different and brand-new person, I'm going to buy a brand-new wardrobe!"

"Right!" Brittany turned back to the rack, flipping through some sweaters. "Hey," she said after a minute, "how about this?"

"I'm not sure about the style," Nikki said, "but I love that blue. I'll try it on."

A few minutes later she emerged from the fitting room wearing a tight royal blue sweater cut very low in the back.

"It's not my usual style," she said doubtfully, turning in front of the mirror.

"It looks great with your eyes," Brittany told her. "And the angora is absolutely beautiful. It's so soft."

"Why not?" Nikki said at last. "I love it."

"Listen," Brittany said quickly. "I have a skirt that would be perfect with that sweater. You can stop by my house on the way home and try it on. I'd be glad to lend it to you."

Nikki hesitated for a moment. Shopping with Brittany was one thing, but borrowing her clothes was another. Evidently, Brittany wanted to make friends with her. Nikki wasn't sure how she felt about it, but, well, borrowing a skirt couldn't hurt.

"Thanks, Brittany," she said. "If it fits, consider it borrowed."

The next morning when Nikki stepped onto the school bus, she was once again the

focus of all eyes. All *male* eyes, at least.
This time, it wasn't because of the incident
during the summer. It was because of the
sweater.

"Wow, Nikki," Lacey said when Nikki sat
down next to her. "I can almost see the tan
line from your swimsuit. You look great,
though," she added quickly.

Lacey was wearing a puffy-sleeved, high-
necked dress in a pretty flowered print. Her
red hair was unbraided, floating around her
face in a mass of waves and curls. "You look
great, too," Nikki said. "I take it Rick likes
your hair down."

Lacey nodded, her pale face growing pink.
"He says it looks like a cloud at sunset. Isn't
that romantic?"

"Oh, he's getting poetic!" Nikki teased.
Then she smiled. "That must mean he's
crazy about you."

"I hope so," Lacey said dreamily. Then
she looked back at Nikki again. "You sure
weren't kidding when you talked about getting a new wardrobe. That's new, too, isn't
it?" she asked, eyeing the short, tight-fitting
black skirt Nikki was wearing.

Nikki shook her head. "It's Brittany
Tate's. Can you believe it?" Then she filled
Lacey in on the shopping expedition. "I can
see why Brittany's so popular," she finished.
"She's got so much energy and spirit."

"She's not always nice, though," Lacey said.

"Well, she sure was friendly yesterday," Nikki said. "I got the feeling that she really wanted to be friends. It was a little weird, since she never wanted anything to do with me before."

"People change," Lacey said. "Rick sure did, so I guess Brittany can, too."

"Well, I don't believe it," Robin put in from the seat behind them. She snorted skeptically.

"Brittany Tate has not changed her spots," she stated flatly. "If she was being nice, she was doing it for a reason."

"Of course she was," Lacey told her. "She wants to be friends with Nikki."

Robin shook her head, her long black earrings swinging against her neck. "She's had years to be friends with Nikki," she pointed out. "And yesterday was the first time she ever did anything about it. Why'd she decide to do it then? That's the real question."

"We'll probably never know the answer, so let's forget it," Nikki told her. "I admit it's all a little strange, but I don't think it's anything sinister. All she did was go shopping with me and lend me her skirt."

"That's *hers?*" Robin's eyes narrowed. "This is getting very suspicious."

"You have a suspicious mind, that's all," Lacey told Robin.

Nikki shook her head, laughing. The two of them could argue forever. "Just tell me one thing," she said as they arrived at school. "Do I look okay?"

"I was going to ask you where the party was," Robin said dryly. "But if you mean 'okay' as in stopping traffic, then the answer is yes."

"You look wonderful, Nikki," Lacey said. "It's just that you don't look like yourself, that's all."

Nikki frowned slightly. "Gee, thanks—I think."

The girls said goodbye, and Nikki headed toward North by herself. As she walked, she was aware of boys watching her.

She wasn't stopping traffic, but she wasn't making it move any faster, either.

Once she got inside, the same thing kept happening, and Nikki started to feel slightly uncomfortable. Not that she minded admiring looks. But *anybody* wearing that outfit would have gotten noticed, she realized. Instead of making her feel special, it made her feel almost as if nobody really knew her. And Lacey did say that she didn't look like herself.

Nikki gave herself a mental shake. Why

was she being so serious? The whole point of buying new clothes and trying different looks was to have fun!

In the hall she spun the combination to her locker and laughed when Jeremy Pratt, the preppy king, walked by and did a double take.

"Uh, hi, there, Nikki," he said.

Nikki grinned. Was Jeremy actually losing some of his cool? He was standing there looking a little ridiculous with his mouth hanging open. "Well, hello, Jeremy," Nikki replied sweetly. Jeremy ought to try a new look himself, she thought, but he cared too much about his image to do that.

She took out the books she needed for the first part of the day, pushed the locker door shut with her knee, and started down the hall toward 101 North.

"Nikki?"

She'd almost plowed into Tim Cooper. Nikki started to smile but stopped when she saw his face.

Tim was ghostly pale. Shaking his head as if to clear his vision, he slowly looked her up and down, taking in the black flats and stockings, the tight-fitting skirt, and the blue sweater. Then he swallowed—hard.

"Are you okay?" Nikki asked, peering into his eyes.

"Sure. It's just that for a minute there you reminded me of—"

"Of what?"

"Nothing." He drew in a long breath. "Listen, there's something I wanted to ask you. You remember how you offered to show me around, sort of help me get to know River Heights?"

Nikki nodded. She hadn't forgotten. But she'd spent most of the day before hoping he wouldn't take her up on it. She was still a little wary of his motives and of her own judgment. Now, though, looking at him, she found herself hoping that he *would* take her up on it. He was so good-looking, and he seemed so nice, that she knew she'd be disappointed if he told her to forget it.

"Well," Tim went on, "I was just wondering if you might want to start—like tomorrow, maybe, after school."

Nikki felt her lips curve into a big grin. "I'd like that a lot."

"Perfect," Tim said, his eyes lighting up. "I'm really glad. Man, for a second there you looked as if you were trying to find a way out of it."

How ironic, Nikki thought. If he'd asked her the day before, she probably would have been.

7 ～

Brittany discussed the shopping trip with Kim and Samantha later that day as they rode home on the bus.

"You've lost your mind!" Samantha said.

"Samantha's right," Kim agreed. "Of all the crazy stunts you've pulled, this one tops them all. You slit your own throat."

Brittany leaned back in the bus seat and laughed. "Au contraire."

"But it doesn't make sense," Samantha said, shaking her head. "I always thought Nikki was pretty, but you made her look ultra sexy. All the boys are going bug-eyed, and I do mean *all.*" She shot Brittany a knowing look. "That includes Tim Cooper."

Smiling mysteriously, Brittany gazed out

the window. Was it time, she wondered, to tell her friends about the letter and the picture of Yvette? And about her plan? No, she decided. Not yet. They might let the cat out of the bag.

"Of course Nikki looked sexy," she said finally. "That's what I wanted." And in spite of their questions and pleas she refused to say anything more.

Later, when she got home and shut herself in her room, she lay on her bed and went over the plan again. She knew it was never good to feel *too* sure of herself, especially not at this stage of the game. One little slip, and the whole thing could backfire. But the plan seemed foolproof. She'd checked it out a hundred ways for flaws and couldn't find a single one.

Smiling confidently, Brittany got up and was just about to change her clothes when there was a tap on her door.

"Brittany?" It was her sister, Tamara. "You'd better come outside, quick!"

"Who says?"

"Me!" Tamara shrieked through the door. "I mean it! It's important!"

Only mildly interested, Brittany opened the door. In the hall stood Tamara— thirteen, super-smart, and a royal pest. She had Brittany's thick dark hair and pretty mouth, but her eyesight was worse than a mole's and she refused to get contacts. She would be a knockout, Brittany thought, if she didn't have to wear those thick-lensed, geeky-looking glasses.

"Okay, what's so important?" Brittany demanded. "If you got me out of my room for nothing, I swear I'll erase every one of your floppy disks!"

Brittany had found that the best way to deal with her sister was through intimidation. Unfortunately, Tamara was too smart for that to work very often. Plus, she had been Brittany's sister for thirteen years. She knew almost every one of her tricks.

Tamara ignored Brittany's threat. "You're not going to believe this!" she cried.

"Believe what?"

"Guess."

"Tamara!" Brittany was getting truly annoyed. "Stop playing games and tell me."

"I'll give you a hint," Tamara said, her eyes twinkling with glee. "It's a present—for you."

Brittany's frown disappeared. "What?"

"It's something you've been dying to have—"

"Tamara!"

"Okay, okay," Tamara relented, and grabbing Brittany's arm, she dragged her down the hall to the front door. "Look!" she said, flinging open the door and pointing outside. "Dad bought you a car!"

Brittany's gaze followed the direction of Tamara's finger. There, at the end of the driveway, was the worst-looking automobile she had ever seen. It was made of metal and had tires and windows, but any resemblance to the car of her dreams ended there. This car was badly dented, and the dents were covered with patches of brown putty. Its hood was wired shut with red electrical cord. Even the antenna was twisted.

Trailed by Tamara, Brittany stepped outside and walked slowly toward the monstrosity. As she drew closer, her father got out of the car, a pleased and expectant grin on his face. "What do you think, honey?"

Brittany felt faint. What could she say? If she drove this wreck around, she'd be a laughingstock.

"It doesn't look like much right now," her dad admitted, "but don't worry. We'll fix it. A tune-up, a little body work, some paint— it'll be as good as new."

"She hates it," Tamara said. "I can tell."

Mrs. Tate emerged from the house, a dish towel in her hands. "Tamara, please," she warned.

"No, I don't," Brittany lied with a gulp. "It's just that—it needs so much work! I'll never get to drive it."

"Sure you will," her father answered. "In fact, the engine's not in bad shape at all. You can drive it to school tomorrow."

Mrs. Tate was smiling. "Isn't that wonderful, dear?"

The thought froze Brittany's blood. "No way! I mean, how will you be able to work on it if I'm driving it around?"

"Oh, I'll do a little at a time," Mr. Tate said happily. "Evenings, weekends. Here, let me show you what I've got planned . . ."

As he opened the hood and began to point out the engine's features, a lump rose unexpectedly in Brittany's throat. She felt like crying. Not because the car was awful. It was worse than awful. She felt like crying because this was, she realized, the sweetest thing her father had ever done.

Impulsively, she hugged him with all her might. "Wow, thanks, Dad. You really are the best, you know that?"

He hugged her back. "You're welcome, Brittany. I'm glad you're pleased, honey."

Proudly, he slid into the driver's seat and started the engine. It didn't exactly roar to life, but it did start right up, and it only wheezed a little. But the way it looked! Brittany simply could *not* take this ugly car to school!

On the other hand, she couldn't insult her father by leaving it at home. After all, he was only trying to give her what he thought she wanted. If she didn't use the car, she'd hurt his feelings.

There had to be a solution, she thought, trying to remain calm. Every problem could be solved, she firmly believed, if she worked on it long enough.

The following morning Brittany was thankful when she saw that the student parking lot was completely empty. That wasn't surprising, as it was only seven-thirty. Even the teachers' parking lot was vacant, Brittany noted with satisfaction as she swung the junkmobile off the main road.

She pulled the car into a space near the entrance. It wouldn't do to park it too close to the road, she figured. The police might mistake it for an abandoned wreck and have it towed.

Brittany climbed out and slammed the door. It didn't close too well, and the lock didn't work, but there was nothing she could do about that. Glancing around again to make sure she hadn't been observed, she started across the lot to the school building. All she had to do now was wait half an hour for the janitors to unlock the main doors. That, and stay awake, she thought with a yawn.

At least she was safe, she consoled herself.

She had driven the car to school, and that had made her parents happy. Even better, there was no possibility whatsoever that anyone would guess it was hers. That made *her* happy.

That afternoon Brittany hid out in the library until four-thirty. She wanted the lot to be as deserted as possible before she climbed into her car.

She also had a lot of thinking to do. It had been an exciting day. Everyone was buzzing with the news that Tim Cooper had asked Nikki Masters out for that night. Brittany couldn't have been happier—her plan was working like a charm. She hoped.

Outside, the air was suffocatingly hot. In her imagination, Brittany was strolling out to her Porsche, getting ready to drive to the country club for a short swim. Of course, her family didn't belong to the country club. They'd been invited to join, but her father thought it was stupid to swim in a pool when they could go to the beach at Moon Lake.

Brittany was a mere ten yards from the junkmobile before she noticed that a crowd was gathered around it. A teacher and a security guard were circling the car, shaking their heads.

"What's going on?" she asked the nearest onlooker.

"Somebody left a wreck," the boy told her.

Brittany began to shake. "Are you sure it's abandoned?"

The boy shrugged. "Pretty sure. Look at it—the thing's falling apart!"

He was right. Sometime during the day, the rear bumper had fallen off. It lay on the ground behind the car like a fossil—a giant chrome dinosaur bone. The tailpipe was also touching the ground, and the muffler was loose.

"See if there are registration papers in the glove compartment," someone suggested.

Brittany gasped—the papers were in her father's name! If anyone found them, they'd know the car belonged to her!

Her heart in her throat, she watched in horror as the security guard tried the driver's door. It wouldn't open. "Locked," he stated.

"No, look! The button's up," someone said. "Let me try."

Brittany recognized the boy: Mark Giordano, the six-foot-three, one-hundred-ninety-pound center on the River Heights football team. Stepping up, he grasped the door's handle in a ham-size fist and shook it. The car rocked back and forth, its springs squealing in protest. Loose parts rattled. The sideview mirror flew off and shattered on the pavement.

Still the door would not open.

The security guard scratched his head. "Well, let's give it until tomorrow. If a student parking sticker isn't on the windshield by then, we'll have it towed."

The crowd began to disperse. Brittany breathed a sigh of relief. She'd gotten a parking sticker from the principal's office that morning; it was in her purse. At least the car wouldn't be towed to a junkyard.

"That sure is a pitiful-looking heap," one boy said as he walked away.

A girl standing next to Brittany nodded. "Can you imagine driving something like that to school?"

"It's horrible," Brittany agreed loudly. "Whoever put it there should be fined!" Several students glanced her way. She smiled at them. She didn't want anyone to suspect—even remotely—that she had anything to do with this eyesore.

Half an hour later, when the parking lots were completely empty, Brittany furtively returned to her car. This time the door opened immediately.

"What's the matter with you, anyway, you pathetic piece of junk?" she grumbled as she slid inside.

A lot, as it turned out. Brittany cranked the starter for fifteen minutes, but the engine wouldn't catch. Blue exhaust floated around the car like a mini-bank of smog.

Finally she gave up. Taking the registration papers, she climbed out, slamming the door angrily—twice. Even then it wasn't fully closed.

"Fine! Stay there! You can rot for all I care!" she yelled. Then she whirled around and began the humiliating march home.

It was almost five o'clock when Tim pulled his car carefully into the parking lot of Strawberry's, a popular hangout not far from the high school. He was a very cautious driver, Nikki noticed. He never tried to make it through a yellow light, never passed even the slowest car, never took his eyes off the road for a second. It was really his mother's car, she reminded herself, and it was brand-new. He was probably nervous about driving it.

Once, on a busy side street, Tim had actually pulled the car over and stopped for a few moments, his face gray.

"What's wrong?" Nikki had asked, alarmed.

"Nothing," Tim had muttered, looking out the car window. "I'm just a little shaky, that's all."

"But why?" Nikki pressed. "Are you sick?"

"No," Tim replied. "I wish those kids would stay on the sidewalk, though. I can't believe their parents are letting them play ball so close to the street.''

Nikki frowned. "Tim, are you *sure* you're okay?"

"Yes," Tim answered. "I'm fine." And with that, he started the engine again.

Nikki was not reassured. Was she making Tim so nervous that he couldn't drive? What was wrong with him, anyway?

Fortunately, Tim's mood lightened as they drove through River Heights.

By now, they'd been driving around for over an hour. Nikki had shown Tim Moon Lake, its clear water shimmering in the late-afternoon sun, and then they'd driven past the country club, the city park, and along the river, of course, where people fished and canoed in the summer. Nikki had pointed out all the popular eating places, and then they had both realized they were starving, so she'd directed him back to Strawberry's.

They ordered Strawberry's famous home-made doughnuts, and Nikki sat back in the booth and looked around. At a crowded booth in the back, she spotted Samantha Daley and Kim Bishop. They smiled and waved, then put their heads together.

Nikki turned back to Tim. He was looking at her eye-catching new gray sweater. Brittany had pointed it out to her during their shopping spree also. A soft, pale wool, it had metallic silvery threads woven in a zigzag pattern across the front, like a flash of lightning.

Their doughnuts arrived, and Nikki took a sip of her tea. "Well," she said, "what do you think of River Heights so far? It's quite a change from Chicago, I guess."

"Yeah, it is," Tim agreed. "But it's a nice-looking town, and it's got some great places. I really like the river." He picked up his cinnamon doughnut and took a large bite. "I really like this doughnut, too," he said with a grin.

Nikki laughed and took a bite of her own doughnut.

They ate in silence for a minute, and then Tim said, "I know I'll get used to the town pretty fast. But getting to know people— that's what'll take time."

"Being new in school must be hard," Nikki said. "Most of the kids are friendly, aren't they?"

Tim nodded. "It's not just them, though. It's me, too," he said. "I mean, they're all as new to me as I am to them. I'm trying to figure out who might be my best—" He stopped suddenly, finished his doughnut, and drank some coffee. "I guess I'm waiting to see who I can trust, and they're doing the same thing. It's natural. But it is lonely while it's going on."

Nikki understood exactly what Tim was talking about. Without hesitating, she found herself telling Tim all about Dan Taylor and how she'd been fooled by his charm. How much she had cared for him at first, only to find that she'd given her trust to the wrong person. Tim was so easy to talk to that it seemed natural to tell him everything.

"It makes me wonder how much to trust other people and myself," she finished.

"You do understand," Tim said. His eyes were sparkling with a mixture of relief and admiration. "I was hoping you would."

Nikki's face colored a little as he gazed at her. His eyes were such an interesting color! "Well," she said, gulping some tea, "I'm glad I didn't disappoint you."

Still watching her, Tim smiled. "I don't think you could do that," he said.

Nikki felt relieved. There was no sign of Tim's earlier moodiness in the car. She wondered what had been bothering him.

At the back of Strawberry's Samantha nodded knowingly to Kim, and the two of them slipped out of their booth. They walked to the pay phone, and Samantha dialed the Tates' number.

"I have some interesting news," she said when Brittany came on the line.

Brittany listened closely, frowning, as

Samantha related the charming little scene between Nikki and Tim. Brittany wanted the two of them to be together, of course—for a while. But this sounded like a little *too* much. Love for Tim and Nikki was not part of her plan.

She'd better move on to Part Two—and fast!

8 ～～

On Saturday morning Nikki stood in the
middle of her bedroom, feeling completely
frustrated. Her room was on the second
floor, overlooking the big backyard with its
velvet green lawn, flagstone walks, and tall
shade trees. Inside, the room was large and
airy, with white walls, sky blue curtains,
golden oak furniture, and several bright,
multicolored modern rugs scattered across
the shiny hardwood floor. Some of Nikki's
best photographs decorated the walls, along
with a big cork bulletin board crammed with
snapshots, invitations, theater programs,
newspaper clippings, lists of things to do,
and a few thousand other items. The bed was
covered with a handmade quilt in vivid

primary colors, but at the moment it was completely hidden by clothes.

Nikki had a date that night with Tim, and she'd just gone through her entire wardrobe, trying to decide what to wear. Nothing seemed right.

She didn't know why the date should be so important. After all, she kept reminding herself, she wasn't in love with Tim.

Still, when they were at Strawberry's, something wonderful had happened between them. They'd talked for almost an hour, swapping stories, sharing jokes, and laughing together like the best of friends.

Friends, Nikki told herself firmly. We're good friends, that's all. So why was she so worried about what to wear?

Just then her bedside phone rang, and she grabbed for it, glad for the interruption.

"Nikki?" It was Brittany Tate.

"Hi," Nikki said, a little surprised. "How's everything going?"

"Not bad. Listen, some of us are going to Leon's tonight," Brittany told her, mentioning a popular high school hangout. "I was wondering if you'd like to come, too."

"Thanks, Brittany, but I can't," Nikki said. "Actually, *I* am going to Leon's, but I have a date tonight with Tim Cooper."

Nikki was kind of curious about how Brittany might react to that information. She had thought Brittany might be interested in Tim. She didn't seem to be anymore, but it was probably best to keep everything out in the open anyway.

Brittany already knew about the date. When Samantha and Kim were leaving Strawberry's, they had overheard Tim ask Nikki. Brittany gritted her teeth, then said breezily, "That should be fun. What are you wearing?"

"That's what I've been asking myself all morning." Nikki laughed. "And I still don't have an answer!"

I do, Brittany thought. "How about a short denim skirt and a plain white T-shirt? There was a model in last month's *Elle* wearing that and she looked fantastic!" She'd also looked a lot like Yvette Weiss.

Nikki had seen that picture, too. "Good idea," she said. "Thanks, Brittany."

"Of course, the key to a simple look like that," Brittany went on, "is the contrast. The plain outfit—with jazzy makeup and hair." Brittany knew exactly how to make Nikki look like Yvette.

"Great," Nikki agreed. "I guess I'll try some fancy stuff."

"Hey, I know!" Brittany made it sound as if she'd just thought of something. "Why don't I come over and help you? I've got everything. It'll be fun." Brittany held her breath.

"Sure, Brittany," Nikki said after a moment's hesitation. "Come over whenever you can."

Brittany smiled into the phone. "I'm on my way."

An hour later Nikki stood in front of her mirror, her just-washed hair hanging in wet clumps. Then Brittany went to work. First, she blow-dried Nikki's hair. Then she heated up the crimper and added some waves. After that, she worked a little mousse into it. "Now," she commanded, "bend forward from the waist, shake your head back and forth, then straighten up and fling your hair back."

Nikki obediently did as Brittany had instructed.

"Now look," Brittany said delightedly.

Nikki looked. The result was incredible. Her eye shadow was a sparkling golden color, and she had on eyeliner and mascara, which made her eyes look huge. Her blond hair was tousled and sexy looking.

Brittany grinned. So far, so good. "Next, some lipstick . . ." She plucked a tube from her purse and handed it to Nikki, who applied it skillfully. It looked perfect.

"Hey, you look as if you just stepped off

the beach at Malibu," Brittany said. Nikki also looked eerily like Yvette.

"Right, and there isn't an ocean within a thousand miles of River Heights!" Nikki agreed with a laugh.

As the front door closed behind her, Brittany sighed heavily. Transforming Nikki into Yvette was one of the hardest things she'd ever done. Not the hair and makeup—that was easy. She looked fabulous. Unfortunately, Tim would think so, too. *That* was the hard part. It was going to be tough that night watching Tim looking only at Nikki.

But it was all part of her plan, Brittany kept telling herself. Part Two was complete. The last part—and the best—was soon to come. Then Tim would be hers.

"Hi, Ni-Nikki?" Tim stood on the front porch of her house. He looked completely astonished.

Nikki laughed. "Who did you think I was?"

"Nobody. I mean—you." Tim ran a hand through his hair. "I mean—what did you do to your hair?"

"I tried a new style." Nikki reached up and touched her tousled mane. "What do you think?"

"I think it's amazing! It's just like . . ." He hesitated.

"Like what?"

"Oh, nothing." Tim shook his head as if to clear it, then grinned at her, his eyes lighting up. "You look spectacular, Nikki!"

Tim wasn't the only one who thought so, either. When they arrived at Leon's, which was a cross between a pizza place and an ice-cream parlor, there weren't many boys who didn't give Nikki a second glance.

Leon's was crowded, so Nikki and Tim wound up sharing a table with Robin, Lacey, and Rick Stratton. After they'd all decided what they wanted, Rick and Tim went to the counter to give the orders.

"Nikki, you look *sooo* gorgeous," Lacey said the minute the three of them were alone.

"I can't argue with that," Robin said. "For once, Lacey and I agree. No wonder Tim can't stop looking at you."

"Thanks," Nikki said, pleased. "Actually, I should be thanking Brittany—she fixed my hair. Don't say it, Robin!" she cried, seeing the peculiar look on her friend's face. "I don't feel like being suspicious tonight. I want to have fun."

"Me, too," Lacey said. "It's not going to be easy, though. Robin's miserable."

"I'm not miserable," Robin protested. "I'm mildly depressed."

"Calvin won't talk to her," Lacey explained.

"He won't?" Nikki was surprised. "I thought you said there was chemistry between you."

"I thought there was," Robin told her. "But I'm beginning to think it's just the real chemistry—as in 'please pass the potassium sulfate.' That's about all he's said to me in three days."

"He's probably just shy and quiet," Lacey told her.

"If he was any quieter, he'd disappear," Robin grumbled.

Tim and Rick came back with the food soon, and the conversation turned to Rick's idea for a hiking club.

"River Heights ought to have one," he said. Rick was medium height, with sandy hair, light eyes, and a brand-new set of muscular shoulders. "Lacey's going to help me get it started."

Nikki and Robin tried not to burst out laughing. Lacey in hiking boots was going to be quite a sight.

After they'd eaten, Rick wanted to get some fresh air, so he and Lacey went for a walk. Robin spotted a couple of kids from the swim team and joined them to discuss an upcoming meet. After she left, Tim and Nikki turned to each other.

He smiled, his glance moving over her face and hair. He liked the way she looked, that was obvious. There was something else in his eyes, but she didn't know what it was. It was making her slightly uncomfortable.

"Nikki," he said, "I want to ask you—"

"Well!" someone said brightly. "Hi there, you two!"

It was Brittany.

Dressed in designer jeans and a flaming red blouse, she smiled at Nikki and Tim as if they were all the closest of friends.

"Nikki, you look fantastic!" Brittany gushed. "You've done something different with your hair, haven't you?"

Nikki bit back a laugh and nodded. You should know, she thought.

"I thought so," Brittany went on. "And your makeup, and—well, it's a whole new look, isn't it?" Without waiting for an answer, she turned to Tim. "I must sound crazy," she said. "But it's just that Nikki looks so different—not like her real self at all."

Tim gave Nikki a curious look, and Nikki felt like squirming in her chair. What does Brittany know about my "real" self? she wondered. And why is she making such a big deal about it?

Nikki was relieved when Brittany left to join her friends, but she suddenly felt terribly uneasy. She knew she was the same Nikki inside, but did Tim know it? Was she sending him wrong signals by changing her style? Ever since she wore that low-backed sweater, he'd looked at her as if she were someone else.

Nikki couldn't shake her uneasy feeling for the rest of the night, and when Tim took her home, she was still worrying.

"Well . . ." Tim said and put his hands on her shoulders. "Nikki, I . . ."

He wanted to kiss her, Nikki knew. She wanted him to. Or did she? Confused, she looked down at her feet. Then she looked up, just in time for his chin to collide with the top of her head.

"Ow!" Tim covered his mouth with his hand. "Sorry," he mumbled. "Bit my tongue." He recovered, laughed, and tried again, successfully this time.

It was a nice, soft kiss. But it wasn't magical for Nikki. For her, the whole date had been spoiled.

"You're crazy not to call him back!" Robin cried. "He's only the best-looking boy in twenty states!"

Nikki held the phone away from her ear while Robin loudly proclaimed Tim's good points. It was three o'clock on Sunday afternoon, and she was still in her bedroom.

"I know he's good-looking, Robin," she said. "And nice and smart and everything else. I just didn't like the way he looked at me."

"Okay, okay." Robin sighed. "You're worried he doesn't know the real you. So let him get to know you."

"I plan to," Nikki said. "Starting tomorrow. No more traffic-stopping sweaters, and no more sexy hairstyles."

When Nikki hung up, she felt a little better. Her "new look" wasn't the only thing that had been bothering her. Every time she was with Tim, she felt more and more as if she was falling for him. But after Dan, she was afraid to trust that feeling. Things had been moving too fast, she decided. From now on, she was going to take it slow.

When Brittany's bus pulled up to school on Monday morning, she hurried to get off, a smug, eager smile on her face. This was The Day. She would put Part Three into motion, then stand back and enjoy the explosion.

As she waited for Kim and Samantha, a crowd of excited kids rushed past, heading for the student parking lot.

"What's going on?" Samantha called out.

"I'm not sure!" one of the kids shouted over his shoulder. "Something about an abandoned car and a big riot with the art club!"

"Come on," Kim said. "Let's go find out."

Brittany bit her lip. This was very, very bad. Her father hadn't been able to come get the car; he'd been tied up at work all weekend. Brittany had come early Saturday morning to try to start it. She'd failed. Fortunately, she'd had the good sense to remove the license plates and stash them in her locker, so the car couldn't be traced to her. Yet.

Her smugness completely gone, and her stomach sinking fast, Brittany followed the others to the student lot. There was no chance the abandoned car in question belonged to anyone else. It could only be hers.

It was.

But it was almost unrecognizable. Draped with crepe paper streamers, artfully spray-painted with colorful swirling designs, it looked like a circus car that had seen better days.

"I tell you, we're going to tow this wreck whether you like it or not!" The school's principal, Edward Meacham, looked frustrated but determined.

A chorus of protest rose from a group of students who had positioned themselves in a protective ring around the car. Brittany knew most of them—they were in the art club.

"No way!" Martin Ives, the club's president, shouted. "We spent most of the week-end decorating it. It's a masterpiece!"

"It's a monstrosity," Mr. Meacham argued.

"It *was*—now it's art!" Sasha Lopez cried. With her spiky dark hair and heavy silver jewelry, she looked like a piece of art herself. "This is a 'found object,' and we demand that you protect it!"

Mr. Meacham threw up his hands in exasperation and turned to a nearby faculty member. "Harry, what are they talking about?"

Paunchy, bald, and sporting a neat goatee, Harry Grotman was chairman of the art department. He was grinning, obviously enjoying the whole thing.

"A 'found object' is a piece of art that isn't created in a studio, but instead is found on the street," he explained. "The artist may or may not modify it. It doesn't matter. It's still art."

"But this isn't art! It's a disgrace!" The principal exploded, pointing to the junk-mobile.

Another roar of protest rose from the students.

The principal narrowed his eyes. "Okay, I'm willing to keep this 'found object' for two days."

"No, no!" the students cried.

"Two days. That's it! After that it's going to be towed." With that, he turned and strode away.

DeeDee Smith, who was standing next to Brittany, looked excited. "This is a great story!"

"I think it's horrible," Brittany said truthfully. "And I agree with Mr. Meacham. That car should be removed. The sooner the better."

"You do?" DeeDee looked at her. "Then why don't you write an editorial about it?"

"I'll be happy to," Brittany volunteered quickly. She was more anxious than ever to separate herself from the car.

"Good. Get it to me right away. We haven't had today's paper printed yet."

Brittany puffed up her cheeks and blew out a long breath. Great! Just great! Editorials were signed by their authors. She'd be going against the art club, and they weren't going to like that at all.

But she couldn't worry about her reputation with the art club. Not when her reputation with the entire school was at stake. She had to do everything she could to get that car out of there.

9

The Record Reacts

All right, the art club had its fun. It took a broken-down eyesore and transformed it into a colorful eye-catcher.

We're talking about the abandoned car, of course. Everybody's talking about it. Unfortunately, after the fun wears off, a lot of people will be shouting about it. Because the student parking lot is for working cars, not eyesores *or* eye-catchers.

It's time for the art club to "find" another object. Art may belong in the streets, but there's no room for it in the student parking lot. . . .

Brittany hurriedly read the editorial she'd just typed on one of the journalism club's rickety machines. Not bad, she thought. Not bad at all. She just hoped it would get the car out of the lot.

She ripped the paper out of the typewriter and rushed across the room to DeeDee, who was busy working on the layout.

"Here's the editorial," she said, "and 'Off the Record,' too." The column had been easy; a new club for teens called Commotion was having its grand opening. Anyone who wanted to be "in" would be there.

DeeDee read both pieces carefully, then nodded. "Good, Brittany." From DeeDee, that was a giant compliment.

But Brittany didn't have time to enjoy it. She'd cut homeroom to write her piece, now she had to take care of another important item: The Plan, Part Three.

Brittany raced through the halls just in time to make it to Nikki's next class.

There she was. And she was obviously in a hurry.

"Nikki!"

"What? Oh, hi, Brittany." Nikki hitched her camera bag higher on her shoulder. "Sorry, I'm kind of late for class."

"Listen, this won't take long," Brittany said. "I just need my lipstick back. You know, the one I lent you on Saturday?"

"Sure, I brought it with me, but I left everything in my locker."

"Well, I really need it," Brittany said. "I forgot mine. Could we go to your locker? But, no, you'll be late. Hmm." She pretended to wonder what to do.

"Oh, here." Nikki ripped a sheet of paper out of her notebook and wrote some numbers on it. "Here's my locker combination. The lipstick's on the shelf. Just make sure you lock the door."

"Don't worry. And thanks, Nikki." Brittany took the piece of paper and watched her dash into the room. Nikki didn't look back as she turned the corner, so she didn't see the triumphant smile on Brittany's face.

The *Record*'s short, back-to-school edition hit the halls just before the last class of that day. By the time the final bell rang, Brittany's editorial was the talk of the school, and to her horror, the car had become a cause célèbre.

"You stirred the art club up even more," Kim remarked as she, Brittany, and Samantha passed the student parking lot after school. "Look at them. They'll never give up now."

Glumly, Brittany admitted Kim was right. Sometime during the day, the car's tires had been removed, and it now sat on four cinder blocks painted in Day-Glo colors. A dozen kids circled it at a steady pace, carrying hand-lettered signs. The signs proclaimed "Freedom of Expression" and "No Censorship." Other kids stood around with petitions, collaring students to sign. Many students were happy to oblige. Too many, Brittany thought hopelessly. And there was Nikki Masters, shooting away with her camera, recording the whole horrible scene.

"Whatever possessed you to write that editorial?" Samantha asked.

"Somebody had to stand up for the rights of working cars," Brittany joked. Thank goodness, Kim and Samantha had no idea the car was hers. If they did, they'd never let her live it down. "I just didn't want the whole thing to be so one-sided," she added, hoping she sounded convincing.

Samantha didn't look convinced, but before she could say anything, Mr. Meacham appeared.

Martin Ives quickly collected the petitions. "There!" he said, handing them to Mr. Meacham. "We've got at least two hundred signatures. And we'll get more. The car is here to stay—the students want it!"

The crowd cheered loudly.

Mr. Meacham scanned the petitions and shook his head. He thought a minute, then raised his hands for silence. "I admire your conviction," he told the crowd. "I disagree with it, but I admire it. So I'm going to call a truce. The car can stay—"

Another wild cheer.

"Until the board of education decides what should be done with it," he went on. "And the board's decision will be final."

The cheers turned to boos, but Brittany felt a surge of hope. The board of education would have to insist that the car be taken away, and then this whole fiasco would be over.

Turning away from the mob scene, Brittany saw Nikki heading back toward the school, camera in hand. Not far behind her was Tim Cooper. Brittany felt a shiver of excitement run down her spine. Nikki might be going to her locker, and Tim would be with her when she did. This could be it, she thought. It could happen now.

"Hey," Tim said, laughing as he caught up with Nikki. "Every time I've seen you today, you've been rushing somewhere. I tried to catch you after homeroom and English, but you outran me."

Nikki laughed, too. Tim was right. She *had* been running all day. She'd even skipped lunch. But she was glad she'd been so busy because it took her mind off Tim.

Now here he was, walking beside her, and there was no more avoiding him.

"I think I missed my bus," Nikki said as they walked along. She had to say *something*. "Oh, well, it's not too long a walk home."

"Maybe I could walk with you," Tim suggested. "If you'd like me to."

As they reached her locker, Nikki stopped and looked at Tim. He was smiling as if he was glad to be with her. He was looking at the real Nikki Masters now—no gold-flecked eyeshadow, no mousse, no tight sweater—and there was no doubt that he liked what he saw.

Nikki's heart suddenly did a funny little flip, and she found herself smiling back. "I'd like that a lot," she said.

"Great!" Tim answered. "There's something else, too. I was wondering if you'd go with me to the opening of Commotion tonight."

Nikki didn't even hesitate. "I'd love to." She smiled again and spun the dial on her locker.

Tim leaned against the next locker and watched her. "I like that top you're wearing," he said.

"Thanks." Good, Nikki thought. It was one of her favorites—soft white cotton with a big floppy collar.

"You know, it's funny," Tim went on.

"Sometimes when I look at you—not today —but a few times before, you've reminded me of—"

Nikki opened her locker and pulled out a stack of papers. "Of what?"

"Not of what, of whom," Tim said.

A notebook and some papers slipped off the shelf and spilled on the floor at Tim's feet.

"Okay, of whom?" Nikki asked.

"Someone I used to go out with back in Chicago." Tim bent to pick up the papers. "She was—"

"She was what?"

Tim didn't answer. He was staring at a folded piece of pink notepaper. As Nikki watched, he slowly unfolded it. Inside was a photograph.

"So that's what happened to it," he said. His voice was quiet. Too quiet, Nikki thought.

She took the note and read it. Then she looked at the snapshot. It was of a girl—a very sexy girl—in a blue low-backed sweater and a tight, skimpy skirt. She was smiling at the camera, her blond hair a tousled mane. Nikki couldn't believe it. She and this girl Yvette could have been twins.

"I've never seen this before," she said to Tim.

"Not even in one of my library books?" he asked. "That's where I left it."

Nikki's mouth was dry. "Tim, I don't know what you're talking about."

"Then how did my letter get in your locker?"

"I don't know," she told him. "But I—"

"You know, it's funny," Tim interrupted. "When I first met you, one of the things I liked was that you were different from any girl I'd ever known. Then all of a sudden you looked like Yvette. Like this picture of her. Now I know why."

"Tim, I—"

"You didn't have to do it," he interrupted again. "I like *you,* not what you were wearing. Why did you pretend to be somebody else? It ruined everything!"

"What?" Nikki cried. "I never lied to you. I didn't steal that letter."

"Okay, you found it," he said. "Whatever. The point is, you didn't tell me. Instead you used the information to trick me."

"No!"

"Come on! I'm not stupid!"

Kids were staring at them. Nikki swallowed hard. Using every ounce of courage she possessed, she forced herself to remain calm.

"Tim, I'll say it once more—I did not take that letter from you," she repeated in a slow, trembling voice. "I never saw it until I opened my locker just now."

"I'm sorry," Tim said, "but I need to

think about this for a while. I guess we'd better forget about Commotion. Thanks for—" He shook his head and walked stiffly away.

Nikki watched him go with her mouth open and her lower lip trembling. The letter was still in her hand.

Any second now, she knew, she was going to start crying.

"Brittany set you up!" Robin said, furious. "I should have guessed!"

"It sure looks that way," Lacey agreed sadly. "Is Brittany the only one who knew your locker combination?"

Nikki nodded.

"Then she was the only one who could have put that letter in." Lacey was so upset her pale face was pink. "How could she?"

"Very easily," Nikki said. "She set a trap, and I walked right into it."

It was late afternoon, and the three of them were in Nikki's room. Nikki had stopped crying, but her eyes were still red.

"Remember—we're not talking about just anyone," Robin reminded them. "We're talking about Brittany Tate. The shark. When she wants something, she zeroes in and doesn't stop till she gets it."

"And she wants Tim," Lacey said.

Nikki paced back and forth, her hands

stuffed in the pockets of her white terry-cloth robe. "But how did she know Tim would be with me?" she asked angrily.

"Don't worry. She had a fall-back plan," Robin said. "With every possibility thought out."

"And I was actually starting to like Brittany," Nikki said.

"That was part of her big scheme," Robin pointed out.

"I guess," Nikki admitted. "Well, anyway, now we know what Brittany did. The question is, what should *I* do?"

"Sneak into her house and stick a skunk in her closet," Robin suggested immediately. "The smell will never come out, and everybody'll know what she really is."

Nikki almost laughed. "I didn't mean Brittany," she said. "I meant, what do I do about Tim?"

"Forget him," Robin said. "He's not worth it. He didn't even give you a chance to explain."

"But he was upset," Nikki pointed out. "And it did look bad."

"Yeah, but—" Robin started to say.

Lacey broke in. "You really like him, don't you, Nikki?"

Nikki nodded, biting her lip. It was so ironic. Just before the awful scene at the locker, she'd felt so happy. He was going to walk her home. He'd asked her to Commotion. She was ready to trust him and trust herself and see what might happen. Now she wouldn't get the chance.

"I really like him," she said softly.

"Then tell him what happened," Lacey urged. "Tell him what Brittany did."

"But I can't prove it," Nikki pointed out.

"No, but at least you can tell him," Lacey insisted.

"Lacey's right," Robin said. "You have to tell Tim the truth."

Nikki took a deep breath. "I'll try," she said quietly.

10 ⤳

"Look at that line! We'll never get in!" Robin moaned.

The line of kids waiting to get into Commotion *was* amazingly long. Commotion was sponsoring a week of special after-school hours to introduce the local high school students to the club. That Monday was for River Heights High only. The club would close early, of course, but that obviously hadn't kept anyone away. Commotion was clearly *the* place to be.

"You sure you're going to be okay?" Lacey asked Nikki.

Nikki nodded. "I feel a little shaky, but I'll make it."

Nikki hadn't wanted to come, but Robin

and Lacey insisted. Robin said if she sat home alone, she'd start crying again and her eyes would be puffy for a week. Lacey thought the crowd and the music would help to take her mind off her troubles. Lacey had planned to go with Rick, but she called and said she'd meet him there, so she could keep Nikki company. Nikki had finally agreed to go.

"Look!" Robin said eagerly. "The line's starting to move!"

Inside, Commotion was every bit as exciting as its advertising had promised. For one thing, it was huge. The dance floor was the size of a warehouse, and it was surrounded by platforms. The sound system pumped out high-decibel music. Lights flashed and strobed; first the mood was soft and romantic, then suddenly it was wild and electric.

Huge black-and-white photos hung from the ceiling. They shared the common theme of "commotion." One showed a screaming mass of people with blank picket signs; another a football scrimmage. Over the nonalcoholic bar hung a blowup of the chariot race in *Ben Hur*. The hall leading to the rest rooms was covered with a life-size mural— Keystone Kops scrambling to escape a runaway railroad engine. Robin loved that one.

The club was an instant success. Within

minutes, the dance floor was jammed. Nikki was amazed at the variety of outfits people had on. Some were in torn jeans and T-shirts. Others wore gowns or rented tuxes.

Nikki had debated long and hard about what to wear. She wanted to look good in case she ran into Tim. She'd finally settled on a snug straight skirt that ended just below her knees. With it she wore a boxy short-sleeved camp shirt. Lacey said she looked terrific — Nikki was just glad she didn't look like Yvette.

The three friends got sodas and stood by the edge of the dance floor to watch the action for a while. In a moment, Ben Newhouse, president of the junior class, cruised up. At his side was a drop-dead-beautiful blond girl named Emily Van Patten. Emily was a junior, but nobody knew her very well. A part-time model, she sometimes traveled to New York and L.A., so she wasn't in school all the time.

"Hi, people!" Ben said cheerfully. "Is this a great place or what?"

Everyone agreed that Commotion was great. Then Emily put her hand in Ben's, and the two of them squeezed onto the dance floor.

"Amazing," Lacey said. "I think Ben's in love."

"He sure looks it," Nikki agreed, watching

Ben's expression as he danced. "So does Emily."

"Ben?" Robin scoffed. "He's been playing the field since sixth grade." She poked Lacey in the arm, smirking. "Speaking of fields, here comes Mr. Outdoors himself."

Rick Stratton, looking extremely uncomfortable, pushed through the crowd to join them.

"Hi," he said. He was wearing a tie and kept twisting his neck as if trying to escape from it. "Not much air in here, is there?"

Robin grinned. "Rick, you look miserable."

"You look wonderful," Lacey told him. Smiling dreamily, she took his hand and they went out to dance.

Watching them, Robin sighed loudly. "At least Rick's here," she complained. "I'll bet Calvin was so busy concocting a new potion, he didn't even see the ads for this place."

"You lose the bet," Nikki said, elbowing Robin in the side. "Look. Calvin's heading this way right now."

Looking nervous but determined, Calvin Roth walked straight up to Robin and cleared his throat. "Robin? Would you like to dance?"

Robin's expression went from shock to delight. "Sure, Calvin! Hey, I'm really glad you're here."

Calvin smiled shyly, and Robin grabbed his hand. "Come on!"

Wistfully, Nikki watched them go. She was glad for Robin and Lacey, but she couldn't help wishing she was out there dancing, too. With Tim. But that might never happen now.

Tears welled up in her eyes, but she gave herself a mental shake. She couldn't start crying right then, right in the middle of Commotion. Besides, Tim might show up. If he did, she was going to make him listen to her side of the story. Part of her was terrified — what if he didn't believe her? But another part couldn't wait for him to get there.

Blinking back her tears, Nikki peered into the crowd, hoping to catch a glimpse of him.

Over by the bar, Jeremy Pratt set down his glass and narrowed his eyes. There was Nikki Masters, all alone. The evening was looking up.

Handsome and spoiled, Jeremy never could figure out why Nikki didn't like him. Oh, she was nice enough to him, but he suspected that was just because she had good manners.

She looked awfully lonely over there all by herself. She looked great, too.

He turned to his buddies, Hal Evans and Wayne Yates. "I think I'll take a stroll."

Straightening the collar of his button-down shirt, Jeremy took two steps and collided with Paul Kelly.

Short, skinny, and eager to please, Paul was the kind of guy who brought out the worst in Jeremy.

"Hi, Jeremy." Paul poked his glasses back on his nose. "Hey, is that your Porsche outside?"

Jeremy nodded, keeping his eyes on Nikki.

"Wow," Paul said. "It's beautiful. I bet the girls are crazy about it, huh?" He smoothed back his unruly hair. "Boy, it must be great to have a car like that. You probably don't even need to say a word, and fifty girls just form a line to get to you." He laughed self-consciously. "I'll be lucky if I can get even one to dance with me."

Jeremy finally turned his gaze on Paul. "Oh, I don't know about that," he said. "I wouldn't be surprised if there were plenty of girls who'd choose you over me." Jeremy wouldn't be surprised; he'd be dumbstruck. "Come on, Nikki Masters is standing over there by herself. Let's both ask her to dance and see who she picks."

"Nikki? No," Paul protested. "She's— I—"

"Come on." Ignoring Paul's stammering, Jeremy took him by the arm and propelled him across the floor. Nikki wouldn't choose Paul, of course. He was no competition at all.

"Nikki," Jeremy said smoothly when he and Paul stopped in front of her, "Paul and I have a problem. We both want you to dance with us, so we thought we'd be gentlemen and let you choose."

"Okay, if you're sure that's the way you want to do it," Nikki said. She smiled and held out her hand to Paul Kelly. "Thanks for asking, Paul. Let's go."

Paul's mouth dropped open. In a daze, he took Nikki's hand.

Jeremy's mouth dropped open, too. Then he saw Hal and Wayne snickering, and he closed it quickly.

As soon as the dance was over, Nikki thanked Paul, got herself another soda, and went back to the same spot she'd been standing in. It had almost been fun, turning down Jeremy Pratt. He was such an incredible snob, she couldn't believe he thought she'd choose him over Paul Kelly.

Of course, she hadn't really felt like dancing—except with Tim. But so far, she hadn't seen him.

Nikki was still standing there, eyes roving anxiously over the crowd, when she felt a heavy hand on her shoulder.

"Hey, pretty girl," a voice said, "how come you're all by yourself?"

Nikki turned and saw a boy with small

dark eyes gleaming at her out of a thick, square-jawed face.

"I don't think I know you," she said, ignoring his question. She moved a couple of steps away.

"Well, I don't know you, either." He laughed out loud and closed the distance between them. "But meeting people's the whole point of this place, right?"

What a creep! Nikki thought. Maybe if she ignored him, he'd go away.

But he had moved and was standing so close that Nikki could feel his breath on her ear. She stepped away again, but he followed. Nikki took a deep breath and counted to ten.

He slipped an arm around her shoulders and grinned. "Looks like it's just you and me, huh?"

Nikki tried to pull away, but his hand tightened on her shoulder. "Come on, don't be shy. Let's have some fun!"

Nikki didn't think; she just turned to face him and then gave him a huge push. He stumbled and looked at her, dumbfounded.

"There," she said. "Is that fun enough for you?"

This time the message apparently got through. Muttering to himself, the boy finally lumbered off.

She'd had enough, she decided. Commotion was a great place, but not for her. Not that night, anyway. She turned to take her glass back to the bar and came face to face with Tim.

"Nikki, are you all right?" he asked. "I saw that guy bothering you. I tried to get over to you, but this place is so crowded that I couldn't move fast enough."

Nikki's heart was pounding and she couldn't think of anything to say. "Yes. I'm okay," she finally managed. "I took care of him."

"Yeah, I noticed," Tim said with a laugh.

He looked fabulous. He was wearing loose-fitting jeans, brown loafers, and a khaki shirt with big front pockets. His gray eyes were sparkling.

"I guess I'll be going," he said, but didn't move.

"Tim, would you do me a favor?"

"Oh, sure!"

A shred of hope flashed through her. Maybe, she thought, the situation wasn't as bleak as she had imagined. She'd expected him to be cold and angry, but he actually seemed glad to see her.

"Can we talk for a minute?" she asked. "I know you're upset with me, but things aren't the way you think at all."

Tim looked doubtful. "Nikki . . ."

"Please!" she said. "I want you to know the truth about what happened."

His features relaxed. "Okay. Let's go where it's quiet."

He led her to a far corner of the lounge off the dance area. It was still noisy, but at least they didn't have to shout.

As they settled onto a plush modular sofa, Nikki tried to frame her thoughts. It was important to keep everything in order and not leave anything out. Once Tim heard her side of it, she was sure he'd see that she was telling the truth. She drew in a breath.

"Tim—"

"Well, hi, there!" a cheerful voice interrupted them.

Brittany! Dazzlingly pretty in a strapless black minidress, Brittany sauntered over as if nothing in the world was wrong.

"Mind if I join you?" Without waiting for an answer, she sat down very close to Tim.

All at once, Nikki was trembling with rage. "Brittany, if you don't mind, this conversation is kind of private."

"Oh, we're all friends," Brittany said lightly. She placed her hand on Tim's knee. "Besides, I'm sure you don't want to make Tim ignore his date all evening, do you?"

His date? Mouth open, Nikki glanced at Tim in disbelief.

Tim's gaze fell to the floor.

Nikki reeled. It couldn't be! It just couldn't! She knew Brittany had framed her in order to make a play for Tim, but she never thought he'd go for Brittany.

With Brittany sitting right there, Nikki knew there was no chance of explaining anything to him. From now on, anything she tried to say against Brittany would seem tinged with spite.

Her heart thudding, Nikki rose to her feet. "I'm sorry. I—I guess this wasn't a very good idea."

Tim leapt up. "No, don't—" Brittany reached out and slipped her hand quietly into his. He hesitated. "Well, that is—if you change your mind about talking, Nikki, let me know."

"Sure."

But Nikki knew she wouldn't change her mind. How could she? Brittany had outmaneuvered her. Brittany flashed her a smile that seemed to say, "You lose! He's mine!"

Nikki couldn't stand it. With tears stinging her eyes, she walked away rapidly and didn't look back.

11

During late study hall the next day, Robin and Nikki were sitting in the student lounge. Nikki was trying to run through her audition speech for *Our Town* after school, but she couldn't concentrate. All she could think about was Tim. And Brittany. Brittany and Tim.

Finally she leaned her head back and sighed out loud. "This is impossible!"

Robin looked up from her trig book. "Nervous?"

Nikki shook her head. "Furious. Depressed. Confused." She sighed again. "I'm a complete mental disaster today. I'll never make it through the audition."

"Sure you will," Robin said. "Just think

how jealous Brittany will be if you get the lead."

Nikki nodded. "But I've got to stop thinking about her. Listen," she said, "I think I'll go out and walk around the halls or something. I'm too nervous to sit still."

Nikki had walked only a short way when she stiffened. Down the hall, Brittany Tate was standing in a classroom doorway. Nikki ducked into another doorway. The last person she wanted to run into in an empty hall right then was Brittany. Nikki peeked around the door frame and realized that Brittany must not have seen her. She wasn't moving in Nikki's direction. She was just waiting.

For what? Nikki stole another glance. She didn't like the expression on Brittany's face. She looked nervous. Extremely nervous, as if she was about to do something scary. Or something *sneaky*. That was much more like it, Nikki thought.

Suddenly Brittany glanced at her watch and then darted off down the hall, away from Nikki.

Glancing back, Nikki saw Robin, who had hooked up with Calvin, coming her way. She crooked a finger for them to join her.

"What is it?" Robin asked when she and Calvin got closer.

"I'm not sure," Nikki said. "But I think Brittany's up to something. Come on."

They waited until they heard Brittany's lone footsteps grow fainter. Then they crept after her. Walking quickly, Brittany made her way to her locker in the North Wing. Nikki, Robin, and Calvin stopped at the connecting door, and Nikki peered through the glass panel.

"What's going on?" Calvin whispered.

"Brittany's just standing in front of her locker," Nikki reported. Then she quickly pulled her head away from the glass panel. "She was looking around. I think she wants to make sure she's alone."

"What could she be plotting this time?" Robin wondered as Nikki sneaked another look.

"She's taking something out of her locker, but I can't tell what." Suddenly Nikki noticed Calvin's camera and camera bag. "Calvin, is there film in that?" she whispered. "And do you have a zoom lens? I want to get some shots of Brittany."

"Yes and yes." Calvin had no idea what was going on, but he was enjoying himself. He quickly took a long, fat lens from his camera bag, screwed it to the camera, and handed it to Nikki.

"Thanks." Stepping up to the glass panel,

Nikki focused the lens and tripped the shutter twice. "Whatever it is, I got it!" she said.

In the school darkroom forty-five minutes later, Nikki unclipped two prints from the line where she'd hung them to dry. Calvin had gone to a science club meeting, but Robin had stuck around. Nikki put the prints on a table, and both girls bent over them.

The first one showed Brittany taking something from her locker. In the second one, Brittany was furtively stuffing something into her book sack.

"It looks like—a license plate."

"*A license plate?*" Nikki was baffled. "The only connection I can imagine is that wreck in the parking lot."

Nikki rummaged in her book sack for the first issue of the *Record*. She found a picture of the decorated car, accompanied by the editorial Brittany had written.

"That car doesn't have plates," Robin said.

"Did Brittany take them off?"

Both girls were puzzled.

"Why would she do that?" Robin asked.

"I don't know, but wait." Nikki searched through a pile of other prints lying on one of the darkroom tables. "I was taking pictures all over the school last week, and I took a few in the student parking lot—*before* the art club members got their hands on that car.

Here they are!" She pulled out the photographs and set them beside the one of Brittany at her locker. "Let's see if the numbers match."

Nikki peered through a magnifying glass. "Uh-huh—it's a match." She handed it to Robin. The license plates that Brittany had taken from her locker exactly matched the ones on the car.

"That joke of a car belongs to Brittany!" Nikki laughed. "And she's the one who says the art club is irresponsible for keeping it around. No wonder she doesn't want anyone to know it's hers."

Robin giggled gleefully. "This is dynamite!" she said. "Now we've got something on Brittany. Once she knows *we* know, she'll have to do whatever we tell her."

"Wait a minute," Nikki said. "Are you thinking what I think you're thinking?"

Robin nodded. "We tell Brittany that we're on to her little secret. Then we promise not to say anything—if she confesses to Tim."

Nikki thought a minute. "I'd love to use it," Nikki admitted. "But . . ."

"But what?" Robin looked frustrated. "Nikki, we've got to do it. Brittany cares more about her image than about Tim, you know she does. If the whole school found out about the car, she'd be the biggest joke around. She couldn't stand it."

"I know."

"Then we've got to show her the pictures," Robin said. "It's the only thing that'll get her to talk."

"Probably." Nikki's mind raced. It was very tempting—using Brittany's secret against her was exactly the kind of sneaky, rotten thing Brittany would do. But this time, Nikki would be the one doing it.

"Well?" Robin asked.

"Oh, I don't know!" Nikki cried. "I can't decide now. And I've got to get to my audition."

"Nikki, you've got to decide."

"I don't know," Nikki called back over her shoulder as she hurried out of the room. "I just don't know!"

By the time Nikki got to the darkened auditorium, the auditions had already begun. Catching her breath, she slipped into a seat and tried to forget about everything except her speech. She wasn't the only one trying out for the part of Emily, the play's romantic lead. Plenty of other girls wanted the role, too. If Nikki didn't concentrate, she wouldn't stand a chance.

She closed her eyes and took a deep breath. When she opened them, she saw Tim sitting a few rows ahead of her.

She didn't realize the boys would be

auditioning at the same time. It was too much. Why didn't the boys wait somewhere else—like Tibet?

When her turn came, Nikki passed Tim on her way to the stage. She suddenly decided: she wasn't going to use the pictures against Brittany. If she did, she'd be doing exactly what Brittany would do, and there was no way she wanted to be like Brittany Tate.

Nikki launched into her audition speech. It began with an angry outburst, and since she was already mad, it was very easy to be convincing. Very quickly, though, as Emily started saying goodbye to everything she loved in life, the stage directions called for her to burst into tears. That was easy, too. Nikki simply let herself go. The pain and betrayal she was feeling came pouring out.

When she had finished, the auditorium was dead silent. Then a few people began to applaud. The drama teacher, Mrs. Burns, made some notes, but all she said was "Thank you. Next?"

Nikki was exhausted. When Tim's turn came, she left quickly.

12 ⟨⟩

A spoon lay on the cafeteria table. Brittany put her fingertip on the bowl and pushed the handle so that it spun around like the minute hand on a speeded-up clock. She was bored —and bothered. Lunch with Tim wasn't going well. He was about as lively as a dead fish. He hadn't said a word to her in nearly five minutes.

"So," she said brightly, "how did your audition go yesterday?"

She might as well have said, "Your dog was hit by a truck." Tim slumped deeper in his chair and groaned. Brittany bit her lip. She knew he was thinking about Nikki, and it burned her up. What could she say that would take his mind off Nikki and put it where it belonged—on her, Brittany?

After all, she loved Tim. She *thought* it was love, anyway. And she wanted him to love her back. She wanted him to find her the most exciting, witty, beautiful girl he'd ever known! Wasn't that the same as love?

But Tim was so lukewarm. He hadn't even asked her to Commotion on Monday—she'd had to do the asking. Ask? She'd practically had to beg, and even then he'd been reluctant to go.

Finally Tim raised his head. "Brittany?"

Brittany straightened up. He was talking to her!

"I have to get going," he said, sliding his chair back. "I want to stop by my locker before my next class."

"Oh—sure." For a second she was tempted to ask him to meet her after school, but she quickly changed her mind. She didn't want to risk being turned down. "See you later," she said, trying to keep her voice light and cheerful.

When Tim had gone, Samantha and Kim hurried over from their table. Kim got right to the point—as usual. "What's his problem?"

"Yeah, the heat was so intense I thought you were going to get frostbite," Samantha added sarcastically.

Brittany tried to think of something witty

to say, but she was tired of pretending everything was great.

"Okay, it's not going so well," she admitted. "He's still getting over Nikki, I guess. Give it time, and pretty soon he'll be ready."

"For you, you mean?" Samantha asked.

"Who else?"

Kim shook her head. "Look, Brittany, your plan was brilliant—capital *B*—but Tim doesn't seem interested in you. As they say, you can lead a horse to water—"

"Brittany Tate?"

An adult voice interrupted them. Looking up, Brittany saw that it was Miss Grannit, the principal's secretary. Her heart began to pound.

"Yes?"

"The principal would like to see you in his office."

It had to be about the car! Her life was over. Finished. Liquidated. Somehow, in spite of everything she'd done to hide it, they'd traced the car to her!

Her heart still pounding in her ears, Brittany followed Miss Grannit out of the cafeteria.

As Brittany walked into Mr. Meacham's office, a wave of panic washed over her. Waiting with the principal were a reporter and a cameraman from WRH-TV. What were they going to do, film the entire humiliating scene?

"Brittany, this is against my better judgment," Mr. Meacham began.

It's against mine, too, Brittany thought. She wished there was some place she could run and hide.

"But Ms. O'Dell, here"—he gestured to the reporter, who was young, blond, and impeccably tailored—"wants to—"

Ms. O'Dell took over. "We're reporting on the controversy over the abandoned car in the student parking lot," she said crisply. "And we need both points of view. Since you wrote an editorial against, we think you're a perfect choice to voice that view."

It took a while for the suggestion to sink in. Even then, Brittany wasn't quite sure she believed it. "You mean, you want to interview me?" she asked.

"Yes, and Mr. Meacham has agreed to excuse you from your next class," Ms. O'Dell said. "What do you say? Is it okay with you?"

It was more than okay, Brittany thought. It was grade-A fantastic!

"Sure!" She gave them all a dazzling smile. What incredible luck!

"Then let's go," Ms. O'Dell said.

They trooped outside. In the parking lot

the car no longer resembled a means of transportation. Each of its body panels had been painted a different Day-Glo color. A papier-mâché mouth was attached to the grille, and dinosaur fins marched up the hood, over the roof, and down the trunk. A tail hung from the bumper. The car looked like a monster that had reared up howling from the sea.

The cameraman switched on his portable light. The reporter held up her microphone and pulled Brittany beside her.

For a brief moment Brittany wondered if she was doing the right thing. She was about to condemn the art club. She was going to demand the principal tow the monster away, when in fact it was *her* monster. Worst of all, the car actually looked better now than it ever had.

But her doubts quickly disappeared. She was going to be on TV! The six o'clock news! Besides, when her father had driven her to school early that morning and tried to start the car, it was dead. Even he had given in and agreed to have it towed.

She owed it to herself to take advantage of this opportunity.

"Tape rolling," the cameraman announced.

The reporter began to speak. "On the

opposing side is student Brittany Tate. Brittany, you feel the so-called found object should be towed away. Why?"

Brittany took a deep breath. "The student parking lot is for cars that work. It's crowded enough as it is. I don't want the art club to think I don't like their project," she went on. "I happen to think it's—attractive. But I wonder how attractive it will be after it rains, when all the decorations get soggy. And after the first big snow, when a plow buries it. It won't be a pretty sight then. In fact, it'll be what it was originally—an eyesore."

"Thank you, Brittany Tate. Reporting from River Heights High, this is Sheila O'Dell, WRH-TV."

That day after classes, Nikki hurried to the auditorium where a crowd was waiting around the bulletin board. The minute the bell rang Mrs. Burns emerged from her office, tacked up a sheet of paper, and quickly scurried back inside to avoid the ruckus.

Students crowded around. Squeals of glee mixed with groans of disappointment. Nikki stood on tiptoe and read the cast list. First on the list were the words: "Emily Webb— Nikki Masters."

She smiled from ear to ear. She had gotten it! The lead role! The next second, though, her spirits sank. Immediately under her name were the words: "George Gibbs—Timothy Cooper."

She and Tim were cast as the play's romantic leads! That meant they would be working side by side every afternoon for weeks.

Nikki stepped back. Behind her, someone coughed loudly. It was Tim.

"Congratulations," he said.

"Same to you," she answered lightly.

"Uh—your audition yesterday was, um, really professional."

"You think so?" She stopped herself. She would *not* get excited. She would *not!* "Thanks. I didn't see yours."

"I know."

They stood awkwardly for a minute, saying nothing. Nikki knew she should walk away. There was no point in torturing herself. She ordered herself to leave, but her feet didn't move.

Finally Tim said, "Look, Nikki—I'm sorry."

"For what?"

"For—for what happened. You know."

Nikki met his eyes. "Does that mean you believe me now?"

Tim was quiet for a long moment. "Well, I want to. Believe me, more than anything in the world I want to! But it's hard. Nikki, can you understand?"

Nikki felt her heart squeeze. She wanted to scream. She wanted to break down and cry. She wanted to shake him by the shoulders and blurt out everything she knew.

"Tim Cooper!" Brittany ran up to him. "I just heard the good news. Congratulations!" She threw her arms around his neck and kissed him on the cheek. "You must be so proud." She turned. "Oh, hi, Nikki," she said easily.

"Nikki got cast as Emily," Tim told her.

"That's nice," Brittany said. She didn't offer her congratulations. She continued speaking to Tim. "So how does it feel? I know the perfect place to celebrate. And guess what? I've got some exciting news, too!"

Nikki shook her head. What a phony! Why couldn't Tim see it? How in the world was she going to get through the next few weeks, rehearsing with him day after day?

She had no idea—no idea at all.

13 ~~~

The next morning at school Brittany was a celebrity. Before she reached the front entrance, a dozen kids stopped her to say they'd seen her on TV.

It was the same inside. One kid after another stopped to talk to her. Brittany floated down the hall, reveling in her instant fame.

She opened her locker and discovered an envelope that someone had apparently slipped in through the vent. Ripping it open, Brittany found a photograph of her car. Except the car hadn't been decorated yet; the picture must have been taken the morning she drove it to school. The license plate was clearly visible, and it was circled in red ink.

Taped to the photograph was a copy of her

Record editorial. In the margin, someone had written, "Who owns this fine automobile? The plates tell all!"

Brittany's blood froze. Someone knew her secret! If this got out, she'd never hear the end of it. She'd be the laughingstock of the school!

Who had put this stuff in her locker?

By the end of her first class, she decided that the culprits had to be Kim and Samantha. This was exactly the sort of thing they would consider a joke. But how had they found out the car was hers? She quickly went over her conversations with them, searching for any telltale slip that might have tipped them off. There was nothing.

Halfway through her second class, another possibility hit her: Tamara, her geeky little sister.

Naturally, Brittany's whole family had found her TV appearance bizarre. It had taken some slick talking to convince them that she hadn't wanted to go on TV, but had done so because no other student was willing to represent the opposing point of view.

They hadn't really believed her, but right now that was the least of her problems. She had to stop Tamara.

Wait, she thought suddenly—how had Tamara managed to get to the high school, sneak inside without being seen, and slip the envelope into her locker? Tamara didn't even know her locker number!

No, it couldn't have been Tamara. It was someone else. But who?

When Brittany went to her locker just before lunch, she found another envelope with another picture. This one showed her sneaking the license plates from her locker into her book sack.

There was a note taped to the picture:

Dear Brittany,

It's not fun to find stuff like this in your locker, is it? If you want the negatives of this picture and of the one you found this morning, you'd better tell a certain guy how a certain letter about his ex-girlfriend got into a certain other girl's locker. . . .

Nikki Masters! Brittany was stunned. It had to be Nikki. For a brief instant, Brittany felt a twinge of admiration for Nikki, but it didn't last long. Nikki had the evidence to make her look like a royal fool.

Would Nikki really carry out her threat? Blackmail wasn't her style. Then Brittany remembered the hurt and anger in Nikki's eyes at Commotion. Maybe she had pushed Nikki just a little too far.

But Nikki's price for her silence was too

high. It was Tim Cooper! And Tim was so important to Brittany—more important than Nikki could ever know.

Or was he? Suddenly she remembered how indifferent he'd been to her at lunch the day before.

Brittany leaned her head against her locker. Tim really was gorgeous. He was also sweet and smart and just about everything else she could want. It would have been nice to have had a relationship with him. Giving him up was going to be very, very difficult.

Nevertheless, she decided it had to be done.

Leaving her locker, Brittany walked quickly to the cafeteria and caught Tim just as he was getting in line. When she said she had something extremely important—and private—to tell him, he agreed to go outside for a few minutes.

As they stepped out the front door of the building, Brittany took a deep breath. "It's about Nikki," she said.

Tim's eyes showed some signs of interest. "What about her?"

"Tim, this isn't easy to say," Brittany told him. "But I just can't stand what's happened with you and Nikki, so I've decided to confess."

"Confess to what?" Tim raised his brows. "Brittany, I don't—"

"The letter," Brittany said in a rush. "I found your letter and the picture of Yvette. I knew how much Nikki liked you, so I didn't tell her about the letter, but I *did* give her a few hints about her clothes and hair."

Tim just stared at her. She couldn't tell what he was thinking. She took another deep breath. "I know I was wrong, and I'm sorry," she said meekly. "But I was honestly trying to help."

"But why? I mean—" Tim shook his head. "How did my letter get in Nikki's locker?"

"Oh, that!" Brittany laughed lightly. "I left it there. I was getting the lipstick she'd borrowed from me, and I set it down and forgot all about it. It was a silly accident."

"Then Nikki was telling the truth the whole time." Tim's handsome face broke into a smile.

Brittany nodded, wishing that his smile could have been for her. "Anyway," she continued, "after I saw how bad things were going between you two, I decided I had to tell you." She lowered her eyes. "I want to help, Tim. I'd do anything to help you, even though you probably hate me now."

"I don't hate you, Brittany."

Brittany looked up. Tim was grinning now. "In fact, I could kiss you!" To her surprise, he leaned over and quickly kissed her cheek. "Thanks, Brittany," he said. "You've helped more than you know!"

Brittany caught her breath. "Oh," she said, startled. "Well, then"—she gave a sudden, dazzling smile—"maybe you could help me."

Tim looked puzzled. "Help you? How?"

"Be my coordinator," Brittany said quickly. "On the halftime show. I need all the help I can get."

Tim hesitated and Brittany smiled harder.

"Okay, sure," Tim said, giving in. "Sounds like fun."

"I'll give you the details later," Brittany promised.

Tim nodded, smiling and moving backward. "Great. I've got to go—right now."

Brittany stayed and thought things over. She'd managed that situation beautifully, she decided. Okay, so she hadn't told the whole truth, but so what? At least she'd saved herself from being exposed as the owner of the junkmobile.

Plus, she didn't have to give Tim up, at least not completely. Now she could really look forward to organizing the halftime show for the alumni football game. Just wait till Nikki found out Tim was working with Brittany. Wouldn't *she* be surprised!

* * *

That same afternoon Nikki headed to the auditorium to be measured for her costume. Afterward she hung around to talk with the other cast members. They were all excited about the show and looking forward to rehearsals.

She was resting in the seventh row—slumped backward, her head against the chair back, her eyes on the ceiling—when Tim abruptly sat down next to her, grinning widely.

"Nikki, I've been waiting all afternoon to tell you something," he said. "I'm a total jerk. I know you'll probably never forgive me, but will you go out with me this weekend?"

Nikki sat up straight and stared. Had he gone completely out of his mind?

"Is this a joke?" she asked.

Tim made a cross over his heart, then raised his palm. "I'm serious! Brittany told me what happened with the letter and everything. Oh, man, Nikki, I can't believe I was so wrong about you!"

"Brittany!"

Tim nodded. "She told me all about taking the letter and coaching you to look like Yvette and how she was only trying to help you."

"Help me?" Nikki repeated. "Brittany told you she wanted to *help* me?"

"Well, to help both of us," he said. "She explained how she left that letter in your locker by accident. And then when she found out I thought you'd taken it, she decided to tell me everything." He gave a wry laugh. "That whole plan of hers was really tricky, and I should be furious, but I'm not. In her own way, I guess she's a pretty good friend."

Tim was practically beaming.

"You think Brittany's a good friend," Nikki repeated slowly. She could hardly believe her ears.

"Yeah, in fact," he added casually, "she asked me to work with her on the halftime show for the alumni football game."

Nikki stared at him, incredulous. Not only had Tim completely fallen for Brittany's lies, but even worse, he was actually going to be working with her! Nikki's cheeks burned. And why had Brittany confessed in the first place? She must have done some real fast talking to come out of this with Tim still liking her.

For a moment Nikki was tempted to tell him how she guessed that that letter had ended up in her locker. But first Nikki had to find out what had caused Brittany's change of heart.

"Stay right there," Nikki ordered him. "Don't move."

She rose and squeezed past him. Marching out of the auditorium, she tore down the hall to the library.

Lacey and Robin were at a table, studying together, books heaped around them.

Nikki sat down and glared at a startled Robin. "Robin, how could you? You blackmailed Brittany! You knew I decided we shouldn't do that!"

"But I didn't blackmail her, I swear!" Robin said. "I wanted to, but I wouldn't go against you, Nikki. Honest!"

"Then what made Brittany tell Tim the truth?"

"She did what?" Robin gasped.

"Well, part of the truth, anyway." Nikki explained what Tim had told her.

"Amazing," Robin remarked. "But I still wasn't the one who blackmailed her."

"Then what happened?"

"I did it," Lacey said suddenly. Her face was pink.

Nikki looked at her in surprise. "You? But, Lacey, why? Didn't Robin tell you what I decided about that?"

Lacey nodded. "Yeah, she did, but I couldn't stand what Brittany did to you. It wasn't right! And you were so unhappy. That was the worst part. You love Tim."

With a start Nikki realized that it was true.

She hadn't admitted it to herself before now—not in those exact words. But it was true, all the same: she loved Tim Cooper.

"Lacey," she said, "all I can say is—thanks!" Smiling, she raced out of the library.

Tim was still waiting in his seat in the auditorium. When Nikki saw him, she felt so happy that she knew she wasn't going to tell him the whole truth about Brittany. Maybe someday, but not now.

"Tim," she said finally, "I'm glad you believe me now, but, well, in a way Brittany was right. I *was* dressing and acting like someone I'm not. It was fun, but it wasn't the real me. I just wanted to tell you that."

"Now can I tell you something?" he asked.

"What?"

"Remember the night you wore your hair just like Yvette's?"

Nikki nodded.

"Well, you knocked me off my feet. You looked really great! And I'm not saying I don't want you to look that way again, but the truth is—well, that's not why I love you."

Love. The word struck Nikki like a cymbal crash. He loved her! He had said it! A symphony was starting in her mind.

"That's great. I mean, I'm—that is, how come?" she managed to ask. Heat was flooding her cheeks. She felt very, very happy.

"Because you're you," Tim said simply. "There are some things about me—well, pretty bad things. I know I can tell you about them someday, but I . . ." His voice trailed away.

Nikki's eyes darkened with concern. "What 'things,' Tim? Can't you tell me?"

"Not now," Tim said quickly. "You never did say if you'd forgive me for not believing you. Will you, Nikki?"

"On one condition," she answered.

"What?"

"That you say it to me." She smiled. "Again."

"You bet!" he said with a grin. "Nikki, I love you."

"And I love *you!*"

He leaned close to kiss her, but Nikki started to laugh. "People are looking at us!"

It was true. All over the auditorium, kids were shooting glances in their direction.

"Let 'em look," Tim said. With that, he leaned even closer and kissed her.

Nikki started to laugh again, but Tim didn't pull away. Sighing, Nikki gave in. She kissed and kissed—and kissed him some more.

She hoped it would feel like this forever,

that nothing would ever go wrong again. But in the back of her mind, a small voice nagged. What "bad things" were in Tim's past?

Squeezing her eyes closed, Nikki pressed her lips against Tim's. Whatever his secret was, she wouldn't think about it now.

Will Tim's hidden past come between him and Nikki? What will Brittany's next move be? Find out in River Heights #2, *Guilty Secrets*.

HAVE YOU SEEN THE NANCY DREW FILES™ LATELY?

# 1 SECRETS CAN KILL	68523/$2.95
# 2 DEADLY INTENT	68727/$2.95
# 3 MURDER ON ICE	68729/$2.95
# 4 SMILE AND SAY MURDER	68053/$2.95
# 5 HIT AND RUN HOLIDAY	64394/$2.75
# 6 WHITE WATER TERROR	64586/$2.75
# 7 DEADLY DOUBLES	62643/$2.75
# 8 TWO POINTS FOR MURDER	63079/$2.75
# 9 FALSE MOVES	63076/$2.75
#10 BURIED SECRETS	68520/$2.95
#11 HEART OF DANGER	68728/$2.95
#12 FATAL RANSOM	68860/$2.95
#13 WINGS OF FEAR	64137/$2.75
#14 THIS SIDE OF EVIL	64139/$2.75
#15 TRIAL BY FIRE	64138/$2.75
#16 NEVER SAY DIE	68051/$2.95
#17 STAY TUNED FOR DANGER	64141/$2.75
#18 CIRCLE OF EVIL	68050/$2.95
#19 SISTERS IN CRIME	67957/$2.95
#20 VERY DEADLY YOURS	68061/$2.95
#21 RECIPE FOR MURDER	68802/$2.95
#22 FATAL ATTRACTION	68730/$2.95
#23 SINISTER PARADISE	68803/$2.95
#24 TILL DEATH DO US PART	68370/$2.95
#25 RICH AND DANGEROUS	64692/$2.75
#26 PLAYING WITH FIRE	64693/$2.75
#27 MOST LIKELY TO DIE	69184/$2.95
#28 THE BLACK WIDOW	64695/$2.75
#29 PURE POISON	64696/$2.75
#30 DEATH BY DESIGN	64697/$2.75
#31 TROUBLE IN TAHITI	64698/$2.95
#32 HIGH MARKS FOR MALICE	64699/$2.95
#33 DANGER IN DISGUISE	64700/$2.95
#34 VANISHING ACT	64701/$2.95
#35 BAD MEDICINE	64702/$2.95
#36 OVER THE EDGE	64703/$2.95
#37 LAST DANCE	67489/$2.95
#38 THE SUSPECT NEXT DOOR	67491/$2.95

Simon & Schuster, Mail Order Dept. ASB
200 Old Tappan Rd., Old Tappan, N.J. 07675

Please send me the books I have checked above. I am enclosing $_____ (please add 75¢ to cover postage and handling for each order. N.Y.S. and N.Y.C. residents please add appropriate sales tax). Send check or money order—no cash or C.O.D.'s please. Allow up to six weeks for delivery. For purchases over $10.00 you may use VISA: card number, expiration date and customer signature must be included.

Name _____

Address _____

City _____ State/Zip _____

VISA Card No. _____ Exp. Date _____

Signature _____ 119-19